MARIANO AZUELA

THE
UNDERDOGS

TRANSLATION AND INTRODUCTION BY

FREDERICK H. FORNOFF

UNIVERSITY OF PITTSBURGH AT JOHNSTOWN

WAVELAND

PRESS, INC.

Long Grove, Illinois

For information about this book, contact:
Waveland Press, Inc.
4180 IL Route 83, Suite 101
Long Grove, IL 60047-9580
(847) 634-0081
info@waveland.com
www.waveland.com

To Carroll Grimes
for her friendship and cheering spirit
over the past thirty years

Contents

Introduction

Mariano Azuela's novel of the Mexican revolution, *Los de abajo*, was first published in 1915 in serial form in the El Paso, Texas newspaper *El Paso del Norte*. He had already published several novels, but none of them had the power of lived experience that so electrifies this enduring masterwork. If you want to write a great war novel, you need to go to war, preferably as an observer or, like Azuela, as a doctor treating the wounded.

Mariano Azuela was born in Lagos de Moreno, Jalisco in 1873, studied medicine in Guadalajara, earned his M.D. in 1899, and practiced medicine until the outbreak in 1910 of the Mexican Revolution, which ended the thirty-year dictatorship of Porfirio Díaz. Subsequently, Azuela supported the candidacy of Francisco Madero, who was elected president in 1911. Following Madero's assassination on February 22, 1913, the reactionary Victoriano Huerta assumed the presidency, and Azuela attached himself as a doctor to the small army of Julián Medina, one of Pancho Villa's generals. He treated the wounded as they moved from Jalisco to Guadalajara to Aguascalientes, usually in retreat from the larger force of Venustiano Carranza, who contended with Villa for control of Mexico after the departure of Huerta for Spain.

Los de abajo derives its vitality and its dialogic quality from Azuela's day-to-day participation in these extraordinary events, observing and interacting with ordinary men who had left their farms to fight for survival in a cause they only dimly comprehended. In the immediacy of his immersion in these events, Azuela found time to write notes complete with snatches of dialogue he surely overheard and to sketch a plot conceived as heroic saga and onto which he superimposed an epic structure. Seymour Menton[1] identified a num-

ber of features that *Los de abajo* has in common with epic poetry—
to mention only three, the association between Demetrio Macías
and Demeter, the Roman goddess of grain; between Demetrio and
Ruy Díaz de Vivar, the hero of the Spanish national epic, the *Poema
del Cid*, in the similar way these two heroic figures gird on their
weapons; and between Demetrio in Juchipila canyon and Roland at
Roncesvalles, both of whom summon their men by blowing a horn.
Menton notes also the similarity between Demetrio's bleak departure from his wife and child early in the novel, the Cid's parting
from his wife and daughters in stanza 16 of the *Poema del Cid*, and
Hector's separation from his wife and son in book 6 of the *Iliad*.

Yet despite these and many other connections with heroic saga,
there is an underside to the action that contrasts sharply with the
courage of Demetrio and his men. The interludes between battles
are marked by uncontrolled looting and debauchery, sharply under-
cutting any idealized representation derived from Azuela's epic
sources. In particular the lewd and cynical character referred to as
the *güero* Margarito and the camp follower *La Pintada* weigh heavily
against the glorification of revolution. In "The Barefoot Iliad,"[2] the
brilliant essay accompanying this translation of Azuela's novel, Carlos Fuentes observes that Azuela's presentation of the seamy side of
the revolution is quite deliberate. Speaking of Demetrio's heroic and
almost single-handed assault on the enemy positions on Bufa peak,
he writes: "But it is precisely here, at the level of epic designation,
that Azuela initiates his devaluation of the Mexican revolutionary
epic. Does Demetrio Macías deserve his epic tag—is he a hero, did
he defeat anyone at Zacatecas, or did he spend the night before the
assault drinking and wake up beside an old prostitute with a bullet
hole in her navel. . . ." Fuentes compares the ruined state of the
towns ravaged by the revolutionary armies to the ruins of Ithaca:
"But Ithaca is a ruin: history destroyed it too. . . . Revolutionary history strips the epic of its mythic support. *Los de abajo* is a journey
from origin to origin, but without myth. And the novel then strips
revolutionary history of its mythic support. This is our profound
debt to Mariano Azuela. Thanks to him it has been possible to write
modern novels in Mexico because he did not allow revolutionary
history . . . to utterly impose itself on us as epic celebration."

Certainly, Azuela's daily contact with Julián Medina's men, whether treating their wounds or simply observing their behavior during and between battles, worked against the characterization of Demetrio's men as purely heroic figures driven by an idealistic urge to transform society. He presents them objectively, and they come alive as human beings because of this. They are men caught up in the maelstrom of revolution, courageous in battle but destructive and stupidly greedy in their looting. They are as oblivious to the artistic value of the treasures they loot as to the transcendence of their own involvement in the revolution. Sentimental and brutal, they are redeemed by their unwavering loyalty to Demetrio, inspired by the virtuous simplicity of his character and the unfathomable sorrow and depth of his authority. In the scene preceding Demetrio's death, his wife asks:

"Why are you still fighting, Demetrio?"

Demetrio, frowning deeply, absent-mindedly picks up a small stone and throws it down into the canyon. He stands there for a moment, staring pensively into the abyss. Then he says, "Look at that stone, how it never stops. . . ."

In this charged moment, Azuela uses the contrast between the small stone and the abyss to suggest the depths and sorrow of Demetrio's character and his near comprehension of the meaning of the revolution.

What good is a revolution? In "The Good Revolution,"[3] an essay written shortly before the Mexican revolution, the Peruvian anarchist Manuel González Prada writes:

> We condemn national revolutions because they impoverish us, dishonor us, bleed us, and turn us into savages. If in normal times the only guarantee of safety rests in the will of the satrap hunkered in his palace, during a civil war the law of Lynch prevails, applied to honest people by criminals. . . . Everyone suffers from abuse of power, those with the least suffering most; thus, the poor Indian ends up crucified between the crook in a frock coat and the brute wearing a poncho.
>
> Our civil wars turn out bad, not because they aren't justified, but because the wicked lead them or take advantage of them. Veritable cannibalistic orgies, they start out with the perpetration of every variety of crime in the provinces and end up

with the execution of three or four thousand men in the streets
of Lima. We erect a mountain of skulls and install at the top a
democratic clown, an androgyne from the Civil Party, or a
three-cornered hat and a sword. . . .

The true popular revolution, the one dreamed of and longed
for by sane men, the one feared and abhorred by the decadent
clowns of politics . . . will come . . . perhaps tomorrow: It won't
be the torrential flood that washes everything away, turning the
fertile fields into a wasteland, but an inundation that will
drown the leeches and spread fecundating alluvial slime over
the impoverished soil. It will be . . . the dawn of the great day.

Notes

[1] "La estructura épica de *Los de abajo* y un prólogo especulativo," *Hispania*, L (1967),
1001–1011; and "Epic Textures of *Los de abajo*," in *The Underdogs* (Pittsburgh and
London: University of Pittsburgh Press in collaboration with Asociación Archivos
de la Literatura Latinoamericana del Caribe y Africana del Siglo XX [ALLCA], a
nongovernmental organization of UNESCO, 1992), pp. 141–155.

[2] This essay, in my translation, was originally printed in the 1992 Pittsburgh/
UNESCO edition of *The Underdogs* (see note 1), and is reprinted here thanks to
the generous permission of Amos Segala, Director of the Archives Collection of
Latin American Literature, who also gave the rights to my translation of *Los de
abajo* for this new Waveland Press edition.

[3] One of the essays from his collection of anarchist writings, *Páginas libres* (*Free
Pages*), to be published in my translation in the Oxford University Press series
Library of Latin America next year.

Note on the Translation

There have been three previous English translations of *Los de abajo*, the first by Enrique Munguía, Jr., in 1930, the second by Beatrice Berler and Frances Kellam Hendricks in 1963, and the most recent by Stanley Robe, published in his excellent study *Azuela and the Mexican Underdogs* (Berkeley: University of California Press, 1979) immediately following his edition of the original text of the novel. Robe's translation is mildly verbose, especially in the dialogue, and seems intended more as an aid to the reading of *Los de abajo* than as a literary equivalent. The two earlier translations are now dated.

In an effort to produce a modern translation that preserves the tone and form of Azuela's novel, I have made several choices. First, I have left intact Azuela's distinctive paragraphing, regarding it as an important key to the novel's striking modernity. Earlier translations conventionalize Azuela's epigrammatic presentation of narrative image and dialogue through standard novelistic paragraphing, which closes off access to the austere simplicity and intensity of the original. Second, I have not attempted to recreate in English the substandard dialect of Azuela's revolutionaries, feeling that the timeless, epic quality of the book is best preserved by using more standard speech. Again, as translations prove, a time- and culture-bound equivalence of low dialect soon becomes outdated. For similar reasons, I have left untranslated certain names and attributes: for example, *güero*, *curro*, *mocho* (see the glossary following the text of the novel).

Third, I have tried to maintain the descriptive spareness that, with the exception of a few deliberately lyrical passages scattered throughout the novel, generally marks Azuela's narrative, imparting remarkable tonal sobriety of the work.

 **The Underdogs**

First
Part

I

"I tell you, that's not an animal. . . . Listen to how Palomo's barking. It must be someone."

The woman peered into the darkness of the sierra.

"You think it's the *federales?*" replied a man who was squatting in a corner eating, a clay bowl in his right hand and three folded tortillas in the other.

The woman didn't answer; she was concentrating on what was happening outside the hut.

Then came the sound of hooves against the rocks nearby, and Palomo started barking more furiously.

"Whether it's them or not, you should hide, Demetrio."

The man, with no change of expression, finished eating; he brought a pitcher to his lips and, holding it with both hands, gulped down the water. Then he stood up.

"Your rifle is under the mat," she said in a low voice.

The small room was lighted by a tallow wick. There was a yoke piled in the corner, a plow, a cane rod and other farm tools. From the ceiling an old adobe mold used for a bed hung down from ropes; a child was sleeping there on blankets and faded rags.

Demetrio strapped his cartridge belt around his waist and picked up his rifle. Tall, powerfully built, of ruddy complexion and beardless, he wore a shirt and trousers of white cloth, a wide-brimmed sombrero woven from palm, and leather sandals.

He stepped outside noiselessly, fading into the impenetrable darkness of the night.

Palomo, furious, had leapt over the corral fence. Suddenly a shot rang out. The dog let out a dull whine and barked no more.

Some men on horseback rode up shouting and cursing. Two of them got down and the other stayed back to watch the horses.

"Women, get us something to eat! Eggs, milk, beans, whatever you have—we're starving!"

"God damned sierra! Only the devil could find his way here!"

"He'd get lost too, sergeant, if he were as drunk as you. . . ."

One of them had chevrons on his shoulders, the other red stripes on his sleeves.

"What's keeping you, woman? . . . Just one? . . . Are you alone in the house?"

"Then why've you got the light on? . . . And that kid? . . . We want to eat, woman, now! You coming out, or do we come in and get you?"

"You bastards! You killed my dog! Why'd you do that? What did my poor Palomo ever do to you?"

The woman appeared dragging the dog, which was very fat and white, his eyes already blank, his body limp.

"Hey, sarge, look at those cheeks! . . . Don't get mad, love, I swear I'll turn your house into a dovecote! Damn!"

> *Don't be so angry . . .*
> *Don't stay mad, bright eyes . . .*
> *Look at me sweetly,*
> *Light of my eyes . . .*

The officer's drunken voice trailed away.

"Woman, what's this place called?" asked the sergeant.

"Limón," the woman answered curtly, stooping to gather up wood and blow on the coals.

"So this is Limón! . . . The land of the famous Demetrio Macías! . . . You hear that, lieutenant? We're in Limón."

"In Limón? . . . Well, the way I see it . . . bah! . . . You know, sergeant, if I'm going to hell, now's as good a time as any, with a good horse to ride. Look what nice cheeks this dark beauty has. I'm going to love sinking my teeth into this peach!"

"You probably know this bandit, woman. . . . I was in Escobedo Penitentiary with him."

"Sergeant, bring me a bottle of tequila; I've decided to spend the night with this honey. . . . The Colonel? . . . Why bring him up at a time like this? . . . Let him go f——! So he gets mad, I could give a . . . bah! . . . Go ahead, sergeant, tell the corporal to take his saddle off and have something to eat. Me, I'm staying here. Here, honey, let my sergeant fry the eggs and warm up the tortillas. You come sit with me. Look, this tight little bundle of bills is all for you. That's the way I want it. What the hell! I'm a little drunk and that's the reason, and that's why my voice is hoarse. The thing is, I left half my guts in Guadalajara and spit the rest out along the way. So what? It's what I want. Sergeant, my bottle, my bottle of tequila. Honey, you're too far away. Come on over here and have a drink. What do you mean, no? You're afraid of your . . . husband . . . or whatever? If he's hiding in some hole, tell him to come out . . . for all I care, bah! . . . I assure you, rats don't bother me."

A white silhouette suddenly filled the dark opening of the door.

"Demetrio Macías!" exclaimed the terrified sergeant, staggering backward.

The lieutenant stood up and stopped talking, frozen in place like a statue.

"Kill them!" exclaimed the woman, her throat dry.

"Ah, forgive me, friend! . . . I didn't know. . . . But I respect real men."

Demetrio stood looking at them, an insolent, scornful smile flickering on his face.

"And I not only respect them, I like them too. . . . Here's the hand of a friend. . . . Okay, Demetrio Macías, go ahead and insult me. . . . That's because you don't know me, because you see me in this shitty job. . . . What do you expect, friend! . . . A guy's poor, he's got a big family to support! Let's go, sergeant; I always respect the home of a brave man, a real man."

As soon as they were gone, the woman embraced Demetrio tightly.

"Holy Mother of Jalpa! What a scare! I thought they'd shot you."

"Go to my father's house, now," said Demetrio.

She tried to dissuade him; she begged, wept; but he replied somberly, pushing her away gently:

"I have a feeling they'll come back, lots of them."

"Why didn't you kill them?"

"I guess their time hadn't come yet."

They went out together, she carrying the child. At the door, they separated, moving off in different directions.

The moon cast mysterious shadows on the mountain. On each crag, on each scrub oak tree. Demetrio stood watching the mournful silhouette of a woman with the child in her arms.

After climbing for hours, he looked back. From the bottom of the canyon, by the river, huge flames were rising. His house was burning. . . .

II

Everything was still in shadows when Demetrio Macías began his descent to the bottom of the ravine. Between the rocky face of the mountain veined with enormous cracks and the cliff hundreds of meters high, a narrow ledge that looked as if it had been carved out with a single stroke served as a path.

As he descended swiftly and sure of foot, he was thinking: *Now for sure the federales will be on our trail. They'll be on us like dogs. Lucky for us, they don't know the trails in and out. Unless someone from Moyahua comes with them as a guide. Because the people from Limón, Santa Rosa and other places in the sierra are loyal. They'd never give us up. The cacique from Moyahua's the one who's got me running through these mountains. He'd like to see me hanging from a telegraph pole with my tongue down to my knees. . . .*

And he reached the bottom of the ravine just as dawn was breaking. He flung himself down among the rocks and slept.

The river dragged along in tiny cascades singing; the little birds chirped from their hiding places in the *pitahaya* cactuses, and the monorhythmic cicadas filled the lonely mountain with mystery.

Demetrio woke up with a start, waded the river and struggled upstream on the other side of the canyon, plodding up crest after crest like an ant, using his hands on rocks and bushes, gripping the pebbles embedded in the path with the soles of his feet.

When he reached the summit, the sun was bathing the altiplano in a lake of gold. Protruding from the sides of the ravine were huge slabs of rock, outcroppings ridged like fantastic African heads; *pitahayas* like the arthritic fingers of a colossus, trees jutting down toward the depths of the abyss. And from the sun-baked crags and dry branches, bright San Juan roses shone like a white offering to the daystar now beginning to slide its golden threads from rock to rock.

Demetrio paused at the summit; he reached back with his right hand; he pulled out the horn hanging at his back, brought it up to his thick lips, and, inflating his cheeks, he blew into it three times. Three whistles answered his signal from beyond the next peak.

In the distance, from behind a conical heap of cane stalks and rotted straw, a group of dark, bronzed men, their chests and legs bare, came out in single file.

They rushed forward to meet Demetrio.

"They burned my house!" he said in response to their inquiring gazes.

They reacted with curses, threats, crude insults.

Demetrio let them vent their anger, then he pulled out a bottle from inside his shirt, drank a little, wiped it off with the back of his hand and passed it to the next man. Once around and the bottle was empty. The men licked their lips.

"God willing," said Demetrio, "tomorrow or even tonight we'll get our chance to look the *federales* in the face again. What do you say, boys, shall we give them a taste of these trails?"

The half-naked men leapt up whooping with joy. Then they renewed the chorus of insults, curses, and threats.

"We don't know how many of them there'll be," observed Demetrio, studying their faces. "Julián Medina, in Hostotipaquillo, with only a half dozen poor devils, armed with knives sharpened on the *metate*, stood up to all the police and *federales* in the village, and chased them out. . . ."

"What have Medina's men got that we don't?" said a powerful-looking bearded man with dark, thick eyebrows and a gentle face.

"All I can say," he added, "is I'm not calling myself Anastasio Montañés anymore if tomorrow I don't get me a Mauser, a cartridge belt, and some trousers and shoes. I mean it! Hey, Quail, you don't look like you believe me. I've got half a dozen bullets in my body already. . . . Ask my buddy Demetrio if that's not so. But I'm about as afraid of bullets as I am of caramel balls. What, you don't believe me?"

"Viva Anastasio Montañés!" shouted Manteca.

"No," replied Anastasio. "Viva Demetrio Macías, our leader, and long live God in heaven and the holy Virgin Mary."

"Viva Demetrio Macías!" everyone shouted.

They made a fire with grass and dry sticks and laid out chunks of fresh meat on the burning coals. They squatted around the flames, hungrily sniffing the meat twisting and sizzling on the coals.

Beside them, the golden hide of a calf lay in a heap on the blood-soaked ground, and sunlight shimmered on the meat drying in the air on a rope strung between two *huizache* trees.

"Okay," said Demetrio. "As you can see, we've only got twenty weapons, not counting my thirty-thirty. If just a few show up, we'll fight until we kill them all; if there are too many, we'll at least give them a good scare."

He loosened the cloth belt around his waist and untied a knot, offering what was inside to his companions.

"Salt!" the men exclaimed excitedly, each one taking a few grains with the tips of his fingers.

They ate ravenously, and when they were full, they stretched out flat on their backs in the sun and sang sad, tuneless songs, letting out wild shrieks after each refrain.

III

The twenty-five men under Demetrio Macías's command slept in the shelter of the sierra underbrush until the sound of the horn awoke them. It was Pancracio signaling from the top of a crag.

"Look sharp, boys! It's time," said Anastasio Montañés, checking the spring mechanism on his rifle.

But an hour passed, with only the sound of cicadas singing in the brush and frogs croaking in the mudholes.

As the glow of the moon faded into the first pink glimmer of dawn, the silhouette of the first soldier appeared at the highest part of the winding trail. Then others appeared, ten more, a hundred more; but they quickly vanished in the shadows. The sun's rays broke through, and the whole side of the mountain was crawling with men: tiny men on tiny horses.

"Look how handsome they are!" exclaimed Pancracio. "Come on, boys. Let's have some fun with them!"

First, the tiny figures would vanish in the chaparral thickets, then they would swarm over the ochre-colored crags, turning them black.

The voices of officers and soldiers rang out clearly.

Demetrio gave a signal: the steel springs of the rifles clicked.

"Now!" he ordered in a low voice.

Twenty-one men fired simultaneously, and as many *federales* fell from their horses. The others, caught off guard, froze in place, like bas reliefs against the rocks.

Another volley, and twenty-one more staggered among the rocks, their brains spilling out.

"Come on out, bandits! . . . Starving dogs!"

"Fucking tortilla-eaters!"

"Kill the goddamn cattle-thieves!"

The *federales* shouted at the silent, unseen enemies who were content to remain in hiding, showing off the marksmanship for which they were famous.

"Watch this, Pancracio," said Meco, the whites of his eyes and his bright teeth shining against his dark skin. "This is for the guy about to pass behind that *pitayo*. . . . Bastard! . . . Got him! Right in the middle of his gourd! Did you see that? . . . Now for the one on the gray horse. . . . Down you go, skinhead!"

"I'm going to give a bath to the one just passing the end of the trail. . . . If you don't make it to the river, *mocho,* you won't miss it by far. . . . How'd you like that? . . . Did you see him?"

"Anastasio, man, don't be a shit! . . . Lend me your rifle. . . . Come on, just one shot!"

Manteca, Quail, and the others who didn't have guns were begging for a turn, as if it would be a supreme privilege to take just one shot.

"Show your faces if you're men!"

"Stick your heads out, you lousy bastards!"

From one mountain to the next, the cries were as clear as if they'd come from across the street.

Quail suddenly stood up, stark naked, prancing around and holding his trousers in front of him like a bullfighter's cape. Then the bullets started raining down on Demetrio's men.

"Shit! It feels like they turned loose a hive of mosquitos around my head," said Anastasio Montañés, flat on his face between the rocks, not daring to look up.

"Quail, you son of a ———! Now everybody move back to where I told you!" roared Demetrio.

And they dragged themselves back to their new positions.

The federales started shouting triumphantly and had stopped firing when a new hail of bullets sent them scrambling.

"There's more of them!" yelled the soldiers.

And, caught up in the panic, many of them turned tail as fast as they could, others jumped off their horses and scrambled up the rocks, looking for a place to hide. The officers had to open fire on their own men in order to restore discipline.

"Get the ones down there! Down there!" yelled Demetrio, pointing his thirty-thirty in the direction of the winding crystalline river.

A federal soldier dropped like a stone into the water, and they kept falling, one by one, with each crack of his rifle. But he was the only one firing toward the river, and for each one he killed, ten or twenty more emerged unscathed on the other shore.

"Shoot the ones down below . . . down there!" he kept yelling, angrily.

His men were passing weapons around now and laying bets on each shot.

"My leather belt if I don't put one in that guy's head, the one on the dark horse. Lend me your rifle, Meco. . . ."

"Twenty Mauser cartridges and half a yard of sausage if you let me drop the one on the bay mare. . . . Okay. . . . Now! . . . Did you see him jump? Like a deer!"

"Don't run away, you fucking *mochos*! Come meet your daddy Demetrio Macías . . ."

The insults were ringing out from Demetrio's men. Pancracio was yelling, his smooth stonelike face extended, and Manteca was screaming, the veins in his neck standing out, the lines in his face stretching down from his fierce murderer's eyes.

Demetrio kept firing while warning the others of the grave danger; but they paid no attention to his desperate voice until they heard the spatter of bullets from their right flank.

"Shit, they got me!" screamed Demetrio, and gritting his teeth he snarled: "Sons of bitches!"

And, wasting no time, he slid down into a ravine.

IV

Two were missing: Serapio the candy maker and Antonio, who played the cymbals for the Juchipila band.

"Let's see if they show up later on," said Demetrio.

Their spirits were low as they made their way back. Only Anastasio Montañés, with his sleepy eyes and bearded face, kept his gentle look, and the lack of expression on Pancracio's hard profile with his protruding jaw was as repulsive as ever.

The *federales* had retreated, and Demetrio was retrieving the horses they'd left hidden in the sierra.

Quail, who had been walking in front, suddenly cried out: he had just spotted the two missing men swinging from the branches of a mesquite. It was Serapio and Antonio, unmistakably. Anastasio Montañés murmured a prayer:

"Our Father, who art in heaven . . ."

"Amen," muttered the others, their heads bowed and their hats on their chests.

And, picking up the pace, they headed north up Juchipila Canyon, not stopping to rest until long after dark.

Quail stayed very close to Anastasio. He couldn't erase from his mind the silhouettes of the hanged men swaying gently in the wind, necks limp, arms hanging down, legs rigid.

The next day Demetrio awoke complaining of his wound. He couldn't get back on his horse. After that, they had to carry him on a stretcher they'd put together with oak branches and clumps of grass.

"It's still bleeding a lot, Demetrio, old friend," said Anastasio Montañés. And with a yank he tore the sleeve off his shirt and knotted it tightly around the thigh, above the wound.

"Good," said Venancio, "that'll stop the bleeding and ease his pain."

Venancio was a barber; in his village he pulled teeth, cauterized wounds, and performed bleedings. He enjoyed a certain prestige because he'd read *The Wandering Jew* and *El sol de mayo*. They called him

"Doc" and he spoke sparingly, with a certain smugness that came from his knowledge.

Spelling each other in groups of four, they carried the stretcher over bare, rocky mesas and up steep slopes.

At midday, the rhythmic, monotonous moans of the wounded man merged with the incessant song of the cicadas and the blinding, suffocating heat rising up from the soil.

At every hut hidden among the jagged rocks they would stop and rest.

"Thank God! We always find a compassionate soul and a tortilla stuffed with chili and beans!" said Anastasio Montañés with a belch.

And the mountain folk, after squeezing their calloused hands warmly, would exclaim:

"God bless you! May he help you and keep you on the right path! You're on the run now; tomorrow we'll be running too, fleeing from the recruiters, hounded by those government bastards. They've declared war to the death on the poor; they steal our pigs, our hens, and even the little bit of corn we've saved to eat; they burn our houses and carry off our women; and, in the end, wherever they catch up with us, right there they finish us off as if we were rabid dogs."

At dusk, when the sky was afire with vivid colors, darkness spread over a group of broken-down houses built on the side of the blue mountain. Demetrio had them take him there.

It was just a few miserable straw huts scattered along the bank of the river amid small fields of newly sprouted corn and beans. They lowered the stretcher to the ground, and in a weak voice Demetrio asked for a drink of water.

In the dark doorways of the huts numerous figures appeared wrapped in skirts of undyed wool, their chests bony, hair disheveled, and behind them, bright eyes and ruddy cheeks.

A chubby boy with dark, glowing skin came out to see the man on the stretcher; then an old woman, and finally they all came out to form a circle around him.

A girl with a friendly face brought him a gourd of clear water. Demetrio seized the vessel with his trembling hands and gulped the water down.

"Don't you want some more?"

He raised his eyes: the girl's face was very plain, but there was great sweetness in her voice.

With the back of his hand he wiped off the sweat running down his brow, and turning over onto his side he said wearily:

"May God reward you!"

And he began to shiver with such force that he loosened the legs of the stretcher. The fever had sapped all his strength.

"This damp night air is bad for the fever," said an old woman in a plain wool skirt, barefooted and with a piece of cloth wrapped around her chest for a blouse. Her name was Remigia. She invited them to bring Demetrio into her hut.

Pancracio, Anastasio, and Quail threw themselves down beside the stretcher like faithful dogs hanging on the master's wishes.

The others scattered to look for food.

Remigia offered what she had: chili and tortillas.

"Just think . . . I had eggs, hens and even a goat with her kid; but those blasted *federales* cleaned me out."

Then, cupping her hands, she whispered into Anastasio's ear, "Imagine . . . they even took Señora Nieves's little girl!"

V

Quail opened his eyes and sat up in alarm.

"Montañés, did you hear that? A gunshot! . . . Montañés, wake up."

He shook him forcefully, until he got him to move and stop snoring.

"What the ———! You're starting to get on my nerves! I told you the dead don't come back" muttered Anastasio, half awake.

"A gunshot, Montañés!"

"Go back to sleep, Quail, or I'll slug you. . . ."

"No, Anastasio, I tell you it's not a nightmare. . . . I've forgotten all about the guys they hung. It really was a gunshot; I heard it clearly. . . ."

"A gunshot? . . . Let's have a look; hand me my Mauser. . . ."

Anastasio Montañés rubbed his eyes, stretched his arms and legs lazily, and then stood up.

They stepped outside the hut. The sky was awash with stars and the moon was rising like a sharp sickle. From the other huts there came the confused sound of frightened women, and from outside, where some of the men had been sleeping, the sound of weapons being readied.

"Stupid! You've destroyed my foot!"

The voice rang out clear and distinct in the hollow.

"Who goes there?"

The challenge echoed from crag to crag, over peaks and hollows, until it faded out in the vast silence of the night.

"Who goes there?" repeated Anastasio more loudly, pulling back the bolt on his Mauser.

"Demetrio Macías!" the voice came from nearby.

"It's Pancracio!" shouted Quail joyfully.

Relieved, he rested his rifle butt on the ground.

Pancracio was leading a young man who was covered with dust from the tip of his felt hat to his scuffed shoes. There was a fresh bloodstain on his trouser leg just above one foot.

"Who's this city boy?" asked Anastasio.

"Okay, I've got the watch, and I hear a noise in the brush so I shout, 'Who goes there?' and this guy answers, 'Carranzo' . . . Carranzo? Now there's a rooster I don't know. So stick that 'Carranzo' shit: and I sunk a piece of lead in his hoof."

Smiling, Pancracio turned his smooth face around, listening for applause.

Then the stranger spoke.

"Who's in charge here?"

Anastasio raised his head angrily and looked straight at him.

The young man's tone softened a little.

"Well, I'm a revolutionary too. The *federales* recruited me and assigned me to the ranks; but in the scrape day before yesterday I managed to desert, and I've come all this way on foot, looking for you."

"Ah, he's a *federal!*" several of them interrupted, looking at him in astonishment.

"So, he's a fucking conservative!" said Anastasio Montañés. "So why didn't you put that piece of lead in his eye instead?"

"How'd I know what he was here for? He says he wants to talk to Demetrio, that he's got some things to tell him! . . . But that's no problem, there's plenty of time," responded Pancracio, getting his rifle ready.

"But what kind of savages are you?" blurted the stranger.

And that's all he had a chance to say, because a backhand blow from Anastasio left him flat on the ground with his face bathed in blood.

"Shoot the conservative bastard!"

"Hang him!"

"Fill him with lead, . . . he's a *federal!*"

They were all shouting and howling in excitement, getting their guns ready.

"Shhh . . . shhh . . . hold it down! . . . I think Demetrio's saying something," said Anastasio, calming them.

In fact, Demetrio asked what was going on and had them bring him the prisoner.

"This is an outrage, sir, look . . . look!" protested Luis Cervantes, pointing to the bloodstains on his trousers and his swollen mouth and nose.

"Okay . . . so? . . . Who the hell are you?" asked Demetrio.

"My name is Luis Cervantes. I'm a medical student and also a journalist. Because I spoke out in favor of the revolutionaries, they came after me, caught me and stuck me in a barracks. . . ."

Pancracio and Manteca were highly amused by the account of his adventure, which he continued to detail in a declamatory tone.

"I tried to make myself understood, to convince them that I'm a true coreligionist. . . ."

"Co-what?" asked Demetrio, pulling on one ear.

"Coreligionist, sir . . . that is, I pursue the same ideals and defend the same cause that you do."

Demetrio smiled. "So tell me, what cause is it we're defending?"

Luis Cervantes, flustered, couldn't find the words to respond.

"My, what a sad face! . . . Why beat around the bush? Can we finish him off now, Demetrio?" asked Pancracio eagerly.

Demetrio raised a hand to the lock of hair covering his ear, scratched for a minute, pensive; then, finding no answer, he said;

"Go away . . . the pain's coming back. . . . Anastasio, blow out

the candle. Stick this character in the corral and have Pancracio and
Manteca guard him for me. Tomorrow we'll see."

VI

Luis Cervantes couldn't quite make out the precise form of objects in the semidark atmosphere of the starry night, and seeking the
best place to rest, he plopped his aching bones down on a pile of
damp manure, at the foot of the blurred mass of a *huizache* tree. More
out of exhaustion than resignation, he stretched out full-length
and closed his eyes with grim determination, prepared to sleep until
his fierce guards awoke him or the late morning sun began to burn
his ears. Something like an odd feeling of warmth at his side, then
the sound of deep, coarse breathing caused him to shiver and extend
his arms in a wide circle around him, and his trembling hand closed
on the stiff hairs of a hog that grunted in obvious displeasure at this
intrusion.

There was no way he could get back to sleep, not so much because
of the pain in his injured foot and the sore flesh as because of the
sudden and precise realization of his failure.

Yes: he had failed to appreciate at the proper time the gulf sepa-
rating his skill at handling the scalpel or blasting nefarious bandits
from the columns of a daily newspaper and actually coming out to
find them in their lairs, rifle in hand. He began to suspect his error
one day's march into his new role as cavalry lieutenant. It had been
a brutal fifty-mile march that left him a solid mass of soreness from
hips to knees, as if all his bones had been soldered together. He knew
it for sure a week later, at the first encounter with the rebels. He could
swear with his hand laid reverently on the blessed cross that when
the soldiers pressed their Mausers to their faces, someone with a booming voice had yelled behind him, "Run for your lives!" Heard it so
clearly that his own horse, a spirited and noble steed, seasoned in
combat, had turned tail and bolted, not stopping until the sound
of gunshots could no longer be heard. And it was precisely at sunset,
when the mountain was beginning to come alive with mysterious and
fearsome shadows, when darkness swiftly ascended the slopes. What
could have been more logical than for him to have sought shelter

among the rocks, to rest his body and spirit and try to get some sleep? But the soldier's logic is the logic of absurdity. So, for example, on the following morning his colonel wakes him with sharp kicks and drags him from his hiding place, with his face bruised and swollen. Even worse: his appearance provokes such hilarity among the officers that, weeping with laughter, they unanimously implore pardon for the deserter. And the colonel, instead of having him shot, plants a savage kick on his backside and takes him out of combat, permanently assigning him to K.P.

Such a blatant insult was to bear poisonous fruit. Luis Cervantes from that point on declares himself a turncoat, though for the moment only to himself. The sorrows and misfortunes of the downtrodden start to affect him now; his cause is the sublime cause of a subjugated people clamoring for justice, only justice. He begins to identify with the humble soldier and—what do you know!—a mule fallen dead from fatigue during a day's march in a rainstorm elicits tears of compassion from him.

And so it happened that Luis Cervantes became trusted confidant to the common soldier. There were those who told him of their awful experiences with the *federales*. One, a very serious fellow, who was known for being calm and reserved, told him: "I'm a carpenter; I lived with my mother, an old woman who had been confined to her chair by rheumatism for ten years. At midnight three *federales* rousted me from my house; I woke up in the barracks and went to bed that night fifty miles from my village. . . . A month ago I marched back through there with the soldiers. . . . My mother was under the ground already! . . . I was her only consolation in this life. . . . Now there's no one who needs me. But I swear by God in heaven, these cartridges I'm carrying here aren't for the enemy. . . . And if the miracle occurs (my Holy Mother, the Sacred Virgin of Guadalupe grant me this!) and I manage to join up with Villa . . . I swear by the sacred soul of my mother, those *federales* will pay for this."

Another young man, very intelligent, but a real charlatan who couldn't stop talking, drank constantly, and smoked marijuana, called him aside, and, staring right at him bleary-eyed, whispered in his ear: "*Compadre* . . . those guys, . . . the ones on the other side, . . . do you know what I mean? . . . they ride the best-fed horses from the

North and from other parts of the country, and their harnesses are decorated with pure silver . . . but we, bah! . . . we ride nags only fit for turning the water wheel. . . . Do you hear what I'm saying, *compadre*? They get paid in shining new peso coins; we, they pay us with flimsy paper bills from that murderer Huerta's printing press."

And so it was with all of them; even a staff sergeant confided naïvely, "I'm a volunteer, but I blew it. What in peacetime you can't earn your whole life working like a mule, today you can make in just a few months running up and down the sierra with a rifle strapped to your back. But not with this scum, brother . . . not with them."

And Luis Cervantes, who already shared with the soldiers that hidden, implacable, and mortal hatred for the non-coms, for the officers, and for all figures of authority, felt the final cobwebs falling away from his eyes and thought he could see clearly the final outcome of the struggle.

But look at him now—no sooner has he joined his coreligionists, instead of welcoming him with open arms, they throw him in a pigsty!

It was daylight: the cocks crowed in the huts; the hens roosting in the branches of the *huizache* tree in the corral stirred, opened their wings and puffed up their feathers, and with one leap fluttered to the ground.

He looked at his guards sprawled out on the dung heap, snoring. In his mind the features of the two men from the previous evening reappeared. One, Pancracio, light-complexioned, freckles, smooth of face, protruding chin, the flat, sloping forehead, ears flattened against his skull, his whole aspect bestial. And the other, Manteca, human garbage: sunken, furtive eyes, straight hair falling limply about his neck, covering his forehead and ears; scrofulous lips eternally gaping open.

And once again a shiver ran over his flesh.

VII

Still half asleep, Demetrio ran his hand through the clumps of curly hair plastered across his sweaty forehead toward one ear. Then he opened his eyes.

Now he heard quite distinctly the melodious voice of a woman he had just heard in his dreams, and he turned to face the door.

It was daytime: sunlight filtered through the thatch of the hut. The same girl who last evening had offered him a clay ladle of deliciously cold water (the stuff of his dreams all during the night), now equally sweet and affectionate, came in carrying a basin of milk brimming with rich foam.

"It's goat's milk, but you'll love it . . . Go ahead, try it . . ."

Grateful, Demetrio smiled and sat up; taking hold of the clay vessel, he began to take small sips, without taking his eyes off the girl.

She nervously avoided his gaze.

"What's your name?"

"Camila."

"I like that name, and even more, the way you say it . . ."

Camila turned bright red, and when he reached out to grab her by the wrist, she became frightened and rushed out with the empty bowl.

"No, friend Demetrio," observed Anastasio Montañés seriously; "first you have to tame them. . . . Hmm, you're talking to someone who's had plenty of experience in these things . . . I've got the scars to prove it."

"I feel good, *compadre*," said Demetrio, pretending he hadn't heard. "I had chills, then I sweated a lot, now I woke up feeling great. What's still bothering me is this damned wound. Get Venancio so he can cure me."

"And what do we do with the *curro* I brought in last night?" asked Pancracio.

"You're right! Damn, I'd forgotten!"

Demetrio, as always, had to think and rethink before making a decision.

"Let's see. Quail, come here. Look, there's a chapel about ten miles from here. Find out where it is, then go swipe the priest's cassock."

"But what are you going to do, *compadre*?" Anastasio was shocked.

"If this *curro* came here to assassinate me, it'll be easy to get the truth out of him. I'll tell him I'm going to have him shot. Quail can dress up as a priest and confess him. If he's a sinner, I blast him; if not, I let him go."

"Hmm, what a lot of fuss! . . . I'd drill the guy, right now." exclaimed Pancracio scornfully.

That night Quail came back with the priest's cassock. Demetrio had them bring in the prisoner.

Luis Cervantes, who hadn't slept or eaten in two days, came in with his face emaciated and bags under his eyes, his lips pale and dry. He spoke slowly and haltingly.

"Do whatever you want with me. I guess I was wrong about you people. . . ."

There was a prolonged silence. Then:

"I thought you would welcome someone who came to offer you his help, poor as mine might be. I sure wasn't doing it for myself. . . . Whether the revolution succeeds or fails, I gain nothing either way."

Little by little, he was getting his spirit back, and the pathetic look started to disappear.

"The revolution is for the poor, the ignorant, those who've been slaves all their lives, poor wretches who don't even know that if they're poor it's because the rich convert their tears and sweat and blood into gold. . . ."

"Bullshit! . . . What are we listening to this for? I can't stand sermons!" interrupted Pancracio.

"I wanted to join the sacred cause of the downtrodden. . . . But you don't understand me . . . you people reject me. . . . So, do whatever you want with me!"

"I'm ready to string this rope around your gullet. . . . Look how fat and white it is!"

"Yeah, I know why you came here." Demetrio spoke gruffly, scratching his head. "I'm going to have you shot, what do you think of that?"

Then, turning to Anastasio: "Take him away . . . and if he wants to confess, get him a priest."

Anastasio, impassive as always, gently took Cervantes by the arm. "Come along, *curro* . . ."

A few minutes later, when Quail came in wearing priest's robes, they all burst out laughing.

"Hmm, this *curro* sure does a lot of talking!" he exclaimed. "I'm pretty sure he was laughing at me when I started asking questions."

"But he didn't confess anything?"

"Only what he said last night . . ."

"I have a feeling he's not here for the reason you think, *compadre*," ventured Anastasio.

"Okay. Give him something to eat and keep your eye on him."

VIII

Luis Cervantes, next day, could barely stand up. Dragging his injured foot, he wandered from hut to hut looking for a little alcohol, boiled water, and strips of used clothing. Camila, kind as ever, got him everything he needed.

As soon as he began to wash and dress the wound, she sat down nearby to watch him, brimming over with rustic curiosity.

"Say, who taught you to dress wounds? . . . And why'd you boil the water? . . . And why are you cooking those rags? . . . Look at me, I sure am full of questions! . . . And what's that you're putting on your hands? . . . That's awful! . . . Is that really whiskey? Go on! I thought whiskey was just for colic! . . . Ah! . . . So you were studying to be a doctor? . . . Ha! . . . That's a laugh! . . . Wouldn't it be better to put cold water on it? . . . Little animals in water that isn't boiled? You're making that up! . . . Yuk! . . . Well, I don't see anything!"

Camila kept asking him questions, and with such ease and familiarity that pretty soon she was using the familiar *tú* pronoun.

Absorbed in his own thoughts, Luis Cervantes was no longer listening to her. *Where are all those admirably armed and mounted men who get their wages in pesos of pure gold that Villa's supposed to be minting over in Chihuahua? Bah! A handful of naked, louse-infested ragpickers, one or maybe two riding broken down mares, bones sticking up from neck to tail. Could it be true what the government-controlled press and he himself had charged, that the so-called revolutionaries were no more than bandits joined together now with a splendid excuse to satiate their thirst for gold and blood? Then was everything the apologists for the revolution claimed just a lie? But if the newspapers were still screaming from every headline victory after victory for the federation, a source just arrived from Guadalajara had let it*

slip that Huerta's relatives and friends were abandoning the capital and head-
ing for the port cities, despite the fact that Huerta kept howling, "I'll bring
peace no matter what it costs." So, whether they were revolutionaries or ban-
dits or whatever you chose to call them, they were going to overthrow the gov-
ernment; tomorrow belonged to them; so you had to be on their side, on their
side only.

"No, this time I'm not mistaken," he said to himself, almost aloud.

"What did you say?" asked Camila. "I was beginning to think the cat had gotten your tongue."

Luis Cervantes furrowed his brow and cast a hostile glance at that beskirted monkey, with her bronze complexion, ivory teeth, and wide, flat feet.

"Hey, *curro,* I'll bet you know how to tell stories?"

Luis put on a mean face and walked off without answering.

Utterly enthralled, she followed him with her eyes until his silhouette vanished down the path to the gulley.

So absorbed was she that she started violently when María Antonia, the one-eyed woman who had been spying on her from the next hut, called out: "Hey, you . . . give him some love powders . . . and see if that makes him fall for you!"

"Sure, that's what you'd do!"

"If I liked him! . . . But, yuk! I can't stand these *curros!*"

IX

"Hey, Remigia, lend me some eggs, my hen woke up hatching. I've got some men here who'd like something to eat."

The neighbor woman opened her eyes wide due to the change from the bright sunlight to the shadowy interior of the hut, which was made even darker by the dense steam rising from the stove. But after a few seconds she could make out more clearly the outlines of things and the wounded man's stretcher wedged into the corner, its head touching the shiny, blackened galvanized iron roof.

She squatted down beside Remigia and, casting furtive glances toward the corner where Demetrio was resting, asked in a low voice:

"How's he doing? . . . Better? . . . Great! . . . Look, and so young! But he's still very pale. . . . Ah! . . . So the wound's still open? . . . Listen, Remigia, don't you want us to try to get it to close?"

Remigia, naked from the waist up, has her veined, withered arms stretched out over the stone pestle of the metate, grinding the cornmeal over and over again.

"They might not like it," she answers without interrupting her strenuous labor, and almost gasping for breath. "They've got their own doctor, so . . ."

"Remigia." Another woman comes in bending her bony back to get through the door. "Don't you have some laurel leaves I can use to make a potion for María Antonia? . . . She woke up with a bellyache."

And since, really, she's just looking for an excuse to pry and gossip, she looks toward the corner where the wounded man is lying and, with a wink, asks about his health.

Remigia lowers her eyes to show that Demetrio is sleeping.

"Hey, are you here too, Pachita? I didn't see you when I came in."

"Good morning, and God bless you, Fortunata. . . . How are you feeling this morning?"

"Well, María Antonia's got her period . . . and as usual, cramps."
She squats down right next to Pachita.

"I don't have any laurel leaves, dear," replies Remigia, suspending her grinding for a moment; she brushes from her sweaty face a few strands of hair that have fallen over her eyes, and then she sinks both hands into the meal, lifting out a huge handful of cooked corn which exudes a dark yellowish water. "I don't have any, but go over to Dolores's: she's always got herbs."

"Dolores had to go over there to the meeting at the *cofradía* last night. From what I hear they came for her to help old Aunt Matías's daughter give birth."

"Go on, Pachita, you don't mean it!"

The three old women form an animated circle and, speaking in low voices, begin to gossip with great zeal.

"As sure as there's a God in heaven!"

"Well, wasn't I the first one to say it: 'Marcelina's getting fat, Marcelina's getting fat!' But no one wanted to believe me. . . ."

"Aw, the poor child. . . . And even worse if it turns out to be her Uncle Nazario's!"

"God help her!"

"No, no way it's her Uncle Nazario! It's those god-damned *federales!*"

"Oh, shit! That's how it goes! Just one more ruined girl . . ."

The racket from the old women finally awakened Demetrio.

They hushed for a moment, then Pachita spoke, pulling from between her breasts a young pigeon which opened its beak, gasping for air, "The real reason I came was to bring these cures for the *señor* . . . but since they say there's a doctor caring for him . . ."

"That doesn't matter, Pachita, . . . that's just something to rub on his skin."

"*Señor,* excuse my poor offering, . . . here's a present for you," said the old crone, moving closer to Demetrio. "For hemorrhaging there's nothing better than these . . ."

Demetrio nodded his head with enthusiasm. They'd already placed several loaves of whiskey-soaked bread on his stomach, and though when they took them off steam seemed to rise from his navel, he felt as if there was still a lot of fever there.

"Go ahead, you know what you're doing, Remigia," exclaimed the old women.

From a cane sheath, Remigia pulled out a long curved knife used for cutting prickly pears from the *nopal* cactus; she held the young pigeon in one hand, stomach up, and cut it in half with a single slice as deftly as a surgeon.

"In the name of Jesus, Mary, and Joseph!" said Remigia, crossing herself.

Then, swiftly, she applied the two warm, blood-spurting halves of the pigeon to Demetrio's abdomen.

"Now you're going to feel much better. . . ."

Following Remigia's instructions, Demetrio lay huddled on his side, very still.

Then old Fortunata told her tale of woe. She had a genuine affection for the revolutionaries. Three months ago the *federales* had taken away her only daughter, leaving her in a state of terrible despair.

When she first began talking, Quail and Anastasio Montañés, sprawled at the foot of the stretcher with their mouths open, had raised their heads to listen to her story; but poor Fortunata rambled on so much and stuck in so many details that halfway through Quail got bored and went outside to scratch himself in the sun, and by the time she concluded solemnly, "I pray to God and to the Holy Virgin that you don't leave a single one of those blasted *federales* alive," Demetrio, turned with his face to the wall, feeling much relief from the substance spread on his stomach, was going over in his mind the best route to take to get to Durango, and Anastasio Montañés was snoring like a trombone.

X

"Why don't you have the *curro* take care of your wound, *compadre* Demetrio?" said Anastasio Montañés to his *jefe,* who day after day went on suffering severe chills and fevers. "You should have seen him, he dresses his own wound and is feeling so much better now, he barely limps."

But Venancio protested. He was standing by with his tins of lard and filthy shreds of cloth.

"If anyone lays a hand on him, I won't answer for the consequences."

"Listen, pal, what makes you think you're a doctor? You don't know a damn thing! . . . I bet you can't even remember why you joined us!" said Quail.

"Sure, Quail. One thing I do remember is that the only reason you're with us is because you stole a watch and some cheap rings." Venancio was incensed.

Quail burst out laughing.

"You're the one to talk! . . . You had to beat it out of your village because you poisoned your girlfriend."

"That's a lie!"

"You did! You gave her Spanish fly to get her to . . ."

Venancio's howls of protest were drowned out by the raucous laughter of the others.

Demetrio, his face showing pain, made them stop; then he began to moan, and said, "All right, let's give him a try; bring that student here."

Luis Cervantes came in, uncovered the leg, took a long look at the wound, and then shook his head. The cloth they'd used for a bandage was sunk into a furrow of skin; his leg was swollen and seemed about to burst open. Every time Demetrio moved, he had to stifle a groan. Luis Cervantes cut the bandage, washed the wound repeatedly, covered the thigh over with moist cloth, and bound it up.

Demetrio slept all afternoon and through the night. The next day he woke up very pleased.

"That young fellow's got soft hands," he said.

Venancio quickly interjected, "Fine; but you ought to be aware that those *curros* are like the dampness, they manage to seep in wherever there's an opening. It's those *curros* that have been the ruin of every revolution."

And since Demetrio had a kind of blind faith in the barber's knowledge, the next day, when Luis Cervantes came in to tend his wound, he said to him, "Hey, do it right so when I'm well again you can go back home or wherever you're headed."

Luis Cervantes, discreetly, didn't say a word.

A week passed, two weeks; the *federales* were showing no signs of life. Besides, there were plenty of beans and corn in the nearby huts; the people hated the *federales* with such intensity that they were delighted to provide food and shelter to the rebels. So Demetrio's men didn't mind waiting for the complete recovery of their leader. For many days, Luis Cervantes remained depressed and silent.

"Hey, *curro,* looks to me like you're in love!" said Demetrio jokingly one day after his daily treatment. He'd begun to grow fond of him and little by little was taking an interest in his well-being. He asked him if he was getting his share of meat and milk. Luis Cervantes had to tell him that he only ate what the kind old women from the huts felt like giving him and that the men still regarded him as an outsider, an intruder.

"They're all good guys, *curro,*" replied Demetrio. "You just have to know how to handle them. Starting tomorrow, you'll get whatever you need. You'll see."

And, in fact, that very afternoon things started to change. Stretched out on the rocks at dusk, staring at clouds that looked like gigantic blood clots, some of Macías's men were listening to Venancio narrate entertaining episodes from *The Wandering Jew.* Many of them, lulled by the barber's mellifluous voice, began to snore; but Luis Cervantes, very attentive, spoke up emphatically as Venancio concluded his performance with wild anticlerical remarks.

"Wonderful! You're really talented!"

"I'm not bad at all," replied Venancio with conviction. "But my parents died, so I couldn't take up a profession."

"That's no problem. With the triumph of our cause, you'll easily get a degree. Two or three weeks working in the hospitals, a good recommendation from our leader Macías, . . . and just like that, you're a doctor. . . . You're smart enough, it'll be a snap for you!"

From that night on, Venancio stopped calling him *curro*. It was Luisito this, Luisito that.

XI

"Say, *curro,* I wanted to tell you something . . . ," said Camila one morning, as Luis Cervantes headed for the hut to get boiled water for his foot.

The girl had been upset for several days, and her flirting and coyness had ended up annoying the young man, who suddenly stopped what he was doing, stood up, staring her right in the face, and asked: "Okay. . . . What is it you want to tell me?"

Then Camila became tongue-tied, and she couldn't utter a word; her face grew red as a beet, she shrugged her shoulders and lowered her head until it was touching her bare breast. Then, motionless and staring at the wound with the blank obstinance of an idiot, she blurted out in a weak voice:

"Look how nice and red it's getting! . . . It's like a rosebud from Castile."

Luis Cervantes frowned with obvious irritation and started dressing his wound again, ignoring her.

When he finished, Camila had vanished.

For three days there was no sign of her. Her mother, Agapita, was the one who came to the door when Luis knocked and who boiled his water and the strips of cloth. He was very careful not to ask questions. But after three days there was Camila again, more coy and coquettish than ever.

Luis, distracted, encouraged Camila with his indifference, and at last she spoke.

"Hey, *curro*, . . . I wanted to tell you something. . . . Listen, *curro*; I want you to teach me "La Adelita" . . . so I can . . . I bet you don't know why? . . . Well, so I can sing it lots of times, lots, when you all go away, when you aren't here anymore, . . . when you're so far, far away . . . that you don't remember me anymore . . ."

The effect of her words on Luis Cervantes was like a steel knife scraping the side of a glass bottle. She didn't notice, though, and went on as naïvely as before.

"Come on, *curro*, I shouldn't have to tell you! . . . You should see what a bad guy your chief is. . . . Let me just tell you what he tried with me. You know how that Demetrio doesn't want anyone but my mama to cook for him and how he won't let anyone but me bring him his food? . . . Okay, well, the other day I was taking the crushed chocolate corn drink in to him and, what do you think the old devil did? Well, he grabs my hand and squeezes it hard, very hard; then he starts pinching my behind. . . . Ah, but I slap him good! . . . 'Hey, quit that! . . . Be still! . . . Stop it, you nasty old man! Let me go . . . let go, you ought to be ashamed!' And then I turn around and slip away . . . and I take off like a bat out of ———. What do you think of that, *curro*?"

Camila had never seen Luis Cervantes laugh so heartily. "But, is what you're telling me really true? Did he really do that?"

Profoundly upset, Camila was unable to respond. He broke out laughing loudly once again and repeated his question. And she, feeling even more upset and anguished, answered in a trembling voice:

"Yes, it's true. . . . And that's what I wanted to tell you. . . . And doesn't it even make you upset, *curro*?"

Once again Camila stared adoringly at Luis Cervantes's fresh and radiant face, those gentle, pale blue eyes, cheeks as bright and pink as a porcelain doll's, his skin so smooth and white and soft beneath the collar and above the shoulders of his coarse woolen poncho, his hair soft and blond and gently curled.

"So what the hell are you waiting for, then, silly? If the chief likes you, what more could you want?"

Camila felt something rising up in her chest, something moving into her throat and forming a knot there. She closed her eyelids tightly to squeeze out the tears welling up in her eyes; then she wiped her wet cheeks with the back of her hand and, as she had three days ago, darted off as lightly as a young deer.

XII

Demetrio's wound had now healed. They were beginning to make plans for marching north, where it was said the revolutionaries had made inroads all along the line against the *federales*. Then something happened to speed things along. One day Luis Cervantes was sitting on a crag in the cool of the afternoon, staring into the distance, day-dreaming. At the foot of the narrow rock, sprawled out among the ironwood shrubs along the river, Pancracio and Manteca were playing cards. Anastasio Montañés, who was watching the game without much interest, suddenly turned his soft eyes and black beard toward Luis Cervantes and said to him:

"Why so sad, *curro*? What are you thinking about so hard? Come on over, let's chat . . ."

Luis didn't move; but Anastasio went over and sat down beside him in a friendly way.

"You miss the excitement of the city, I can tell. You're a sharp guy, a fellow who's used to wearing shined shoes and fancy shirts. . . . Look at me, *curro:* you see me, all dirty and ragged, but I'm not really that way. . . . All right, you don't believe me. . . . I'm not here because I have to be; I've got ten yoke of oxen all my own. Really! . . . Just ask my *compadre* Demetrio. . . . I've got my half acre of farmland. . . . You don't believe me, do you? . . . Look, *curro;* I enjoy harassing the *federales,* that's why they're after me. Last time, about eight months ago (that's when I joined up with these guys), I cut up one of their cocky little captains (God help me), stuck a knife right here, right in the belly. . . . But, really, I don't have to be here. . . . I'm here because of that . . . and just to help out my buddy Demetrio."

"There's the beauty I was looking for!" shouted Manteca, overjoyed with the card he'd drawn. He put a twenty-centavo silver coin on the jack of spades.

"Would you believe, I don't care much for gambling, *curro*! . . . You want to place a bet? . . . Go ahead, have a look; this little leather snake's still jingling!" said Anastasio, shaking his belt to make the peso coins clink together.

Then Pancracio dealt the cards, turned up the jack and a quarrel broke out. Complaints, shouts, then insults. Pancracio jutted his stony face out toward Manteca, who stared at him with viperous eyes, his face convulsed like that of an epileptic. They looked as if they were about to swing at each other. Unable to come up with any more biting insults, they started in on each other's mother and father, weaving a rich tapestry of foul language.

But nothing happened; when they had run out of insults, the game was over, and they walked off together calmly in search of a shot of whiskey, arms flung over each other's shoulder.

"That's another thing I don't like, fighting with words. That's ugly, don't you agree, *curro*? . . . Really, look, no one's ever insulted my family. . . . I like to have people respect me. That's why you'll never see me going around shooting off my mouth. Hey, *curro*, take a look," continued Anastasio, changing the tone of his voice, shielding his eyes with his hand and standing up. "What's that cloud of dust over there, behind that little hill? Damn! It's got to be the *federales*! . . . And here we are, not even ready for them! Come on, *curro;* we've got to let the boys know."

The news caused great rejoicing.

"Let's go get them!" Pancracio was the one who started it off.

"Yeah, let's go after them. Whatever they bring with them, we'll take it!"

But the enemy turned out to be just a bunch of burros and two muledrivers.

"Stop them. They're from the mountains and they're bound to have some news," said Demetrio.

And in fact they had some sensational news. The federal troops had fortified Grillo and Bufa, the two hills overlooking Zacatecas. Rumor had it this was Huerta's last stand, and everybody was predicting the fall of the city. The residents were leaving in a hurry, head-

ing south; the trains were overcrowded; there were hardly any carriages or carts available, and hundreds of panic-stricken people were
hurrying along the main road, carrying their possessions on their
backs. Pánfilo Natera was gathering his men in Fresnillo, and the
federales were acting as if they knew it was all over.

"The fall of Zacatecas will be the *Requiescat in pace* for Huerta,"
proclaimed Luis Cervantes with unexpected conviction. "We need
to get there before the assault and join forces with General Natera."

And noticing the quizzical looks his words brought to the faces
of Demetrio and his men, he realized he was still a nobody there.

But the next day, when the men went out in search of some good
mounts for resuming the march, Demetrio called Luis Cervantes over
and said to him:

"Do you really want to go with us, *curro?* . . . You're made of
different stuff from us, and, really, I don't see how this life can appeal
to you. You think we do this for the sheer pleasure of it? . . . Well,
sure, why deny it? . . . we like the excitement; but it's not only
that. . . . Sit down, *curro,* sit down so I can tell you. You know
why I joined up? . . . Look, before the revolution I already had my
field plowed, and if it hadn't been for that run-in with Don Mónico,
the cacique from Moyahua, right now I'd be rushing about, getting
my oxen yoked for the planting. . . . Pancracio, get us two bottles
of beer, one for me and one for the *curro.* . . . By the Holy
Cross . . . this can't do us any harm, can it?"

XIII

"I'm from Limón, over there near Moyahua, right in the middle
of Juchipila Canyon. I had my house, my cows, and a nice piece of
land to farm; so you see, there was nothing I needed. Well, we farm-
ers usually go into town once a week. You go to mass, you listen
to a sermon, then you go to the square, you buy some onions, some
tomatoes, all the things on the list. Then you and your buddies go
over to Primitivo López's store around eleven. You have a drink or
two; sometimes just to be sociable you let down a little and the drinks
get to you, and you start enjoying yourself, you laugh, you shout
and sing, if that's what you feel like doing. It's just fine, because you're

not bothering anyone. But maybe they start to mess with you; the cops keep passing by, just looking for trouble; maybe the chief of police and his deputies take a notion to spoil your fun. . . . Hey, friend, that's blood running through your veins, not soda pop, and you've got your soul right there in your body where it belongs, and you get a little mad, so you stand up and tell them exactly who you are! If they understand, well and good; they stop bugging you, and that's it. But sometimes they get pushy and start to talk tough . . . so you start throwing it right back at them . . . because you don't back down for anybody. . . . And sure enough, out comes a knife, or a pistol! . . . And then you're heading for the hills until everyone's forgotten about some jerk you've killed!"

"Okay. What happened with Don Mónico? That asshole! Really almost nothing compared to some of the other times. There wasn't even any blood spilled! . . . All I did was spit in his face for bothering us, and you can guess the rest. . . . Well, that's all it took to get the whole federal government on my case. You probably heard about what happened in Mexico City, where they killed Señor Madero and another guy, Félix or Felipe Díaz, something like that, how should I know! . . . Okay, so this Don Mónico went in person to Zacatecas to get a squad of soldiers to take me in. He told them I was a Maderista and that I was going to start a revolution. But, you know, a guy's got friends, so someone told me in time, and when the *federales* came to Limón, I'd already taken off. Later on my *compadre* Anastasio came along with me, after he killed somebody, and then Pancracio, Quail, and a lot of friends and people I knew. After that, more guys joined up, and as you can see: we're carrying on the fight as best we can."

After several minutes of silence and meditation, Luis Cervantes spoke:

"*Jefe,* you know that some of Natera's men are close by, in Juchipila; it would be a good idea to join them before they take Zacatecas. We should introduce ourselves to the general. . . ."

"That's not my style. . . . I don't like to bow down to anybody."

"But just you alone, with a few men from around here, you'll never be more than just some small-time *jefe,* of little importance. The revolution is going to triumph, without fail; as soon as it's over, they'll tell you, the way Madero told those who helped him: 'Friends, thanks a lot; now return to your homes. . . .'"

"That's exactly what I want, to be left alone to return to my home."

"Hold on . . . I'm not finished: 'You men, who carried me all the way to the presidency of the republic, risking your lives, with the very real danger of leaving behind widows and orphans in misery, now that I've attained my goal, go gather up your shovels and hoes, go back to living half dead, always hungry and poorly clothed, the way you were before, while we, those at the top, rake in a few million pesos.'"

Demetrio shook his head and scratched himself, smiling.

"Luisito just said a mouthful, right from the pulpit!" exclaimed the barber, Venancio, very enthusiastically.

"As I was saying," continued Luis Cervantes, "when the revolution's over, everything's over. Too bad about all those lives lost, all those widows and orphans, all that blood spilled! All for what? So a few scoundrels can get rich and everything stay the same or worse than before. You're pretty detached about it, so you say: 'All I want is to go back home.' But do you think it's fair to deprive your wife and children of the fortune divine Providence is ready to place in your hands? Is it right to abandon your country at this solemn hour when she's going to need every bit of abnegation from her children, the poor, who can save her, keep her from falling once again into the hands of her eternal oppressors and executioners, the *caciques*? . . . You mustn't forget what's most sacred to a man in this world: his family and his country!"

Macías smiled with his eyes shining.

"So, you think it'd be a good idea to go with Natera, *curro*?"

"Not just good," pronounced Venancio in a conspiratorial tone, "but indispensable, Demetrio."

"*Jefe*," continued Cervantes, "I've liked you ever since I first saw you, and I like you more all the time, because I can see how good you are. Let me be completely frank with you. You haven't yet come to understand your true, high, noble mission. You, a modest man, without ambition, prefer not to see the crucial role that's yours to play in the revolution. It's not true that you're here just because of your run-in with Don Mónico, that cacique. You've taken up arms against the very idea of *caciquismo,* which is destroying this nation. We are part of a great social movement whose goal is to make our country great. We are instruments destined to revindicate the sacred rights of the people. We aren't fighting to overthrow some wretched assassin, but against the very idea of tyranny. That's what's called fighting for principles, having ideals. That's why Villa, Natera, and Carranza are fighting; that's why we're fighting."

"Hey! That's exactly what I've been thinking," said Venancio, filled with enthusiasm.

"Pancracio, get us two more beers. . . ."

XIV

"If you could have heard how well the *curro* explains everything, Anastasio *compadre,*" said Demetrio, concerned about what he'd been able to get out of Luis Cervantes's words that morning.

"I was listening to him," answered Anastasio. "Really, now, he's a guy who, because he knows how to read and write, understands things clearly. But what I don't quite get, *compadre,* is how you're supposed to go and introduce yourself to Señor Natera when there're so few of us."

"Hmm, that's no problem! From now on we're going to operate differently. I heard that Crispín Robles goes around to all the villages collecting as many weapons and horses as he can find; he lets the prisoners out of the jails, and in no time he's got men to spare. You'll see. The truth is, Anastasio my friend, we've been pretty dumb. I can't believe some *curro* has to come teach us the ropes."

"That's what comes of knowing how to read and write!"

They both sighed sadly.

Luis Cervantes and the others came in to find out when they were leaving.

"We're heading out tomorrow," said Demetrio with no hesitation.

Then Quail proposed bringing musicians from a nearby little town and having a farewell dance. Everyone welcomed his idea with great enthusiasm.

"Well, we're finally leaving!" exclaimed Pancracio, letting loose with a howl. "But I'm not going alone this time. I've got a girl and I'm taking her with me."

Demetrio said he too had his eye on a girl he'd like to take along, but he didn't want any of them to leave bad feelings behind, the way the *federales* always did.

"You won't have long to wait; when we return everything will be arranged," whispered Luis Cervantes.

"What do you mean?" said Demetrio. "Isn't everyone saying that you and Camila . . . ?"

"There's no truth in that, *jefe;* she likes *you* . . . but she's afraid of you."

"Really, *curro?*"

"Sure; but what you said earlier seems absolutely right: we mustn't leave a bad impression. . . . When we return in triumph, it will all be different; they'll even thank us for looking at them."

"Ah, *curro*! . . . You're a sly one!" responded Demetrio, smiling and patting him on the back.

At dusk, Camila started down to the river for water, as she did every day. Luis Cervantes came walking along the path toward her.

Camila felt as if her heart would leap right out.

Perhaps without seeing her, Luis Cervantes suddenly vanished around the side of a huge rock.

At that time of day, as every day, the calcinated rocks, sun-baked branches, and dry moss took on a softer hue as the shadows spread. A warm breeze was blowing softly, stirring the pointed leaves of the tender ears of corn. Everything was the same as usual; but for Camila now there was something strange about the stones, the dry branches, the warm, perfumed air, and the rustling leaves—as if a great sadness had fallen over everything.

She stepped around the edge of a huge eroded cliff and came suddenly upon Luis Cervantes, sprawled on a rock, his legs hanging over the edge and his head bare.

"Hey, *curro*, at least come say goodbye."

Luis Cervantes was fairly civil. He got down and walked over to her.

"Stuck up! . . . Did I treat you so poorly you can't even speak to me?"

"Why do you say that, Camila? You've been very good to me, better than a friend; you took care of me like a sister. I'm very grateful to you, and I'll always remember you."

"Liar!" said Camila, overcome with joy. "And if I hadn't said anything to you?"

"I was going to thank you tonight at the dance."

"What dance? . . . If there's a dance, I won't go. . . ."

"Why not?"

"Because I can't stand the sight of that old guy . . . that Demetrio."

"Don't be silly! . . . Look, he really likes you; you'll never have another chance like this. Don't pass it up. Silly, Demetrio's going to end up a general, he'll be rich. . . . Lots of horses, rings and bracelets, fancy dresses, elegant homes, and loads of money to spend. . . . Just imagine what it will be like to be at his side!"

To keep him from seeing her eyes, Camila raised them toward the blue of the sky. A dry leaf broke loose from near the top of the cliff and, swaying slowly in the breeze, fell at her feet like a dead butterfly. She stooped down and took it between her fingers. Then, without looking him in the face, she whispered:

"Oh, *curro,* . . . if you could only see how awful it makes me feel when you talk to me like that! . . . You're the one I like . . . but not any longer. . . . Go away, *curro,* go away; I don't know why I feel so ashamed. . . . Go away, go away!"

And she let the pieces of the crushed leaf fall through her tense fingers and covered her face with the corner of her apron.

When she opened her eyes again, Luis Cervantes had disappeared.

She continued down the path to the stream. The water seemed to be dusted with a fine crimson sheen; in its waves she could see a brilliant sky shimmering, and peaks half shrouded in shadow, half blazing with light. Swarms of luminous insects blinked on and off in the deep pools. And mirrored in the clean stones at the bottom, she could see her yellow blouse with the green ribbons, her white, unstarched petticoat, her hair smoothed back to make her eyebrows and forehead look wider—all made up just so in order to please Luis.

And she burst into tears.

In the bushes the frogs were croaking out the implacable melancholy of the hour.

Swaying on a dry branch, a dove wept too.

XV

At the dance everyone was happy and there was lots of good *mezcal* to drink.

"I miss Camila," said Demetrio loudly.

And everyone looked around for Camila.

"She doesn't feel well, she's got a headache," replied Agapita angrily, annoyed by the mean looks everyone was giving her.

As the shindig was ending, Demetrio, staggering slightly, thanked the good people for their warm hospitality and promised to remember them when the revolution triumphed, because, he said, "In bed and in jail a man finds out who his friends are."

"God keep you in his holy hand," said an old woman.

"God bless all of you and keep you on the right path," said others.

And María Antonia, extremely drunk: "Come back soon . . . but I mean real soon!"

The next day María Antonia, who despite her pocked face and an eye that was clouded over had a very bad reputation, so bad that it was rumored that there wasn't a man in the region who hadn't lain with her in the bushes down by the river, shouted at Camila:

"Hey, you there! . . . What's going on? . . . What are you doing in the corner with that shawl over your head? . . . What? . . . Crying? . . . Look at your eyes! . . . You look like a witch! Come on, . . . don't be upset! . . . There's no heartache that lasts more than three days."

Old Agapita squinched up her eyebrows; no telling what she was muttering to herself.

Actually, all the old women were out of sorts because the column had just headed out, and even the men, despite all their insults and boorish remarks, were sorry there wouldn't be anyone to bring in

a lamb or a calf so they could have meat to eat every day. How nice
it is to spend your life eating and drinking, dozing flat on your back
in the shade of the rocks while the clouds bunch up and then scatter
in the sky overhead!

"Look, you can see them again now! There they go," shouted María
Antonia. "They look like toy soldiers!"

In the distance, where the brambles and chaparral seemed to merge
into a sea of bluish velvet, Macías's men on their scrawny nags were
outlined against the translucent sapphire sky as they filed along the
crest. A gust of warm air carried the muffled, broken strains of "La
Adelita" all the way to the huts.

Camila, on hearing María Antonia's remark, came out to see them
one last time, but she couldn't control her emotions and went back
inside choking with sobs.

María Antonia gave a raucous laugh and left.

"They've put the evil eye on my daughter," muttered old Agapita,
perplexed. She thought about it for a long while, and when she had
figured it out, she knew what she had to do: from the stake nailed
to the cornerpost of the hut between the Divine Countenance and
the Virgin of Jalpa, she took down an untanned leather strap her husband used for yoking the oxen and, doubling it, gave Camila a dozen
good whacks to drive out the evil spirit.

Demetrio, sitting on his chestnut-colored horse, felt rejuvenated;
his eyes had recovered their peculiar metallic gleam, and the pure Indian blood was running hot and red once more through his copper-
colored cheeks.

All of them were expanding their lungs as if they wanted to breathe
in the far horizons, the vastness of the sky, the blue of the mountains, and the fresh air sweetened with the smell of the sierra. And
they pushed their horses to a gallop, as if in that unrestrained running they were trying to take possession of the whole land. Who cared
now about some sadistic chief of police or ill-tempered patrolman
or pompous cacique? Who cared now about the wretched hut where
you lived like slaves, always spied on by the owner or some brutal,
angry foreman, under the relentless obligation to be on your feet before the sun comes up, with your shovel and basket, or plow handle

and ox-goad, just to earn your daily bowl of corn mash and a plate of beans?

They sang, laughed, and hooted, drunk on the sun and the air, drunk on life.

Meco, prancing on his horse and clowning around, showed off his white teeth and made jokes.

"Hey, Pancracio," he asked with a straight face. "In this letter my wife sent she tells me we've got another son. How can that be? I haven't seen her since the days of Señor Madero!"

"Don't worry about it . . . it's nothing. She was pregnant when you left!" They all laughed raucously. Only Meco, very serious and seemingly oblivious, sings in a horrible falsetto.

> *I gave her a penny*
> *but she just said no . . .*
> *I gave her a nickel*
> *but she made me feel low.*
> *She kept after my ass*
> *till she got the whole dime.*
> *Ay, these women are bad,*
> *they just waste a man's time!*

The noise died down when the sun began to make them drowsy.

All day long they rode through the canyon, going up and down the round hills, bald and dirty, like an endless succession of soot-covered heads.

Toward dusk, they made out some steeples way off in the distance, halfway up a blue ridge, then the main road, marked by white clouds of dust and the line of gray telegraph poles.

They kept on till they came to the road and saw in the distance the figure of a man squatting beside it. They rode toward him. He was a ragged old Indian with a grumpy expression. He was having trouble, trying very hard to fix one of his huaraches with a dull knife. Nearby his burro was grazing, loaded down with dry grass.

Demetrio asked:

"What are you doing here, old man?"

"I'm taking alfalfa to town for my cow."

"How many *federales* are there?"

"Yeah, just a few. I think there are fewer than a dozen."

The old man began to speak more freely. He said there were some serious rumors: that Obregón had Guadalajara under siege, Carrera Torres had taken San Luis Potosí, and Pánfilo Natera was in Fresnillo.

"Okay," said Demetrio. "You can go on to your village; but don't say a word to anyone about what you've seen, or I'll blast you. I'd find you even if you hid in the center of the earth."

"What do you say, boys?" asked Demetrio after the old man had left.

"Let's give it to them! . . . We won't leave a single one of those conservative bastards alive!" they shouted in unison.

They counted their cartridges and the hand grenades that Owl had made out of lengths of iron tubing and brass knobs.

"We don't have many," observed Anastasio, "but we're going to exchange them for carbines."

And they pressed forward eagerly, digging their spurs into the thin flanks of their exhausted mounts.

Demetrio's commanding voice brought them to a halt.

They camped at the foot of a hill, sheltered by a thick grove of *huizache* trees. Without unsaddling, each of them set out to find a stone for a pillow.

XVI

At midnight, Demetrio Macías gave the order to march. The town was five or six miles away, and they wanted to catch the *federales* by surprise, striking before dawn.

The sky was overcast, with only one or two stars peeping through, and now and then the horizon lighted up in the ruddy glow of a lightning flash.

Luis Cervantes asked Demetrio if it wouldn't be a good idea for them to find a guide, just to improve their chances for a successful attack, or at least try to scout the topographic layout of the town and the exact location of the barracks.

"No, *curro*," replied Demetrio smiling scornfully; "we'll attack when they're least expecting it, and it'll be over. That's how we've always done it. Have you seen the way squirrels stick their heads out of their holes when someone pours water in? Well, that's exactly how confused these miserable government soldiers are going to be when they hear the first shots. They'll come out and we'll use them for target practice."

"And what if that old Indian we questioned yesterday lied? What if instead of twenty soldiers there are fifty? What if he was a spy posted there by the *federales*?"

"This *curro* has gotten cold feet all of a sudden!" said Anastasio Montañés. And Pancracio chimed in: "Yeah, dressing wounds isn't the same thing as handling a rifle!"

"Hmm!" said Meco. "This is a lot of chatter for a dozen frightened rats!"

"This is no time for our mothers to be wondering if they gave birth to men or not," added Manteca.

When they came to the outskirts of the little town, Venancio went on ahead and knocked at the door of one of the shacks.

"Where's the barracks?" he asked the man who came out, barefoot and holding a serape in front of him to cover his bare chest.

"It's right down there, boss, just beyond the square," he replied.

But since no one knew where the square was, Venancio made him walk in front of the column and show them the way.

The poor devil was trembling with fear; he complained that what they were making him do was outrageous.

"I'm just a poor peasant, *señor;* I've got a wife and little kids."

"And you think mine are dogs?" snapped Demetrio.

Then he ordered them:

"Keep very quiet, and go across the open ground one by one halfway down the street."

The broad quadrangular dome of the church loomed over the row of shacks.

"Look, *señores*. The square's in front of the church; just walk on down there a little further, and you'll run right into the barracks."

Then he knelt down, begging them to let him go back; but Pancracio, without a word, smashed him in the chest with the butt of his rifle and made him go forward.

"How many soldiers are there?" asked Luis Cervantes.

"Boss, I don't want to tell you a lie; but the truth, the pure truth, there's a whole army there."

Luis Cervantes turned back toward Demetrio, who pretended he hadn't heard.

Suddenly they were right on the edge of a little square. A tremendous barrage of rifle fire deafened them. Trembling, Demetrio's chestnut-colored horse staggered on its legs, its knees doubled and it fell to the ground kicking. Owl gave a piercing cry and rolled off his horse, which bolted into the middle of the square with its reins hanging down.

Another volley, and the man guiding them spread his arms wide and fell on his back, without even a moan.

Anastasio Montañés stooped down and pulled Demetrio up on his horse behind him. The others had already retreated, looking for shelter behind the walls of the houses.

"*Señores, señores,*" said one of the villagers, sticking his head out of a wide vestibule, "come at them from behind the chapel . . . that's where they're all posted. Go back down this street, take a left turn, then you'll come to a small alley . . . stay on that and you'll end up right behind the chapel."

Just then they were hit by a furious rain of pistol shots. It was coming from the roofs of the adjacent houses.

"Hmm," said the man, "those aren't just flea bites! . . . It's the wealthy townspeople, scared out of their wits! . . . Stay inside here until they clear out."

"How many soldiers are there?" asked Demetrio.

"There weren't but about a dozen; but last night there was a scare, and they wired ahead for reinforcements. Who knows how many there are now! . . . But don't worry even if there are a lot of them. Most of them are recruits, and it won't take much to make them desert and leave the officers alone. My brother got drafted and they've brought him with them. I'll go with you and I'll send him a signal and you'll see how they'll all come over to our side. And then we'll just have the officers to deal with. If the *señor* would just give me a gun . . ."

"There aren't any rifles left, brother; but see what you can do with these," said Anastasio Montañés, handing the man two grenades.

The leader of the *federales* was a young blond with a waxed mustache, very presumptuous. As long as he wasn't exactly sure how many men were attacking, he had kept quiet and been extremely cautious; but now that they had repelled them so successfully that they hadn't even returned fire, he was strutting around with an extraordinary display of arrogance. While his soldiers were barely peeping their heads out from behind the walls of the church portico, he daringly thrust his svelte profile into the pale morning light, and every now and then his hooded cloak caught a breeze and swelled up like a sail.

"Ah, this reminds me of our coup d'état!"

Since his military career had been limited to the episode he'd been involved in as a cadet in Officer's Training School at the time of President Madero's assassination, whenever an opportunity presented itself, he'd find a way to bring up his role in the heroic uprising against Fort Ciudadela in Mexico City.

"Lieutenant Campo," he commanded imperiously, "take ten men down there and give it to those cowardly bandits. . . . Mangy curs! They're pretty brave when it comes to butchering stray cattle and stealing a few chickens, but that's about it!"

One of the townsmen came to the little door leading to the spiral staircase. He brought the news that the rebels were in a corral, where they could be trapped quickly and without much risk. That word came from the prominent citizens of the town, who were posted on the rooftops and eager to keep the enemy from escaping.

"I'll finish them off myself," said the officer impetuously. But then he changed his mind. He stepped back behind the door to the stairs.

"It's possible they're waiting for reinforcements, and it wouldn't be wise for me to abandon my post. Lieutenant Campos, you go and bring them in alive, all of them, so I can have them shot today at noon, while the folks are coming out of mass. Those bandits will find out I know how to set an example! . . . But if that's not possible, Lieutenant Campos, go ahead and kill them. Don't leave a single one alive. Do you understand what I'm saying?"

And he started walking up and down, pleased with himself, thinking about the official report he would turn in: "Your Excellency, Minister of War, General Aureliano Blanquet. Mexico City. It is my great honor, General, to bring to your exalted attention that at daybreak

of such and such a day . . . a force of five hundred men under the
command of H—— had the audacity to attack this town. With the
urgency which the situation demanded, I dug in on the hills overlooking the town. The attack began at dawn, and for more than two
hours we were under heavy fire. Despite the numerical superiority
of the enemy, I succeeded in inflicting severe casualties on them, even-
tually routing them. The number of their dead was twenty, with many
more wounded, judging by the bloodstains they left behind in their
hasty retreat. In our ranks we had the good fortune of suffering not
a single casualty. It is my great privilege to congratulate you, Minister, on the occasion of this victory by the federal troops. Long live
General Victoriano Huerta! Long live Mexico!"

"And then," he continued to daydream, "my certain promotion
to major." And he squeezed his hands together jubilantly, just as a
tremendous explosion left his ears ringing.

XVII

"So if we could cross through this corral, we'd come out right on
the alley?" asked Demetrio.

"Yes; but there's a house just on the other side of the corral, then
another corral and then a store beyond that," replied the villager.

Demetrio, deep in thought, scratched his head. But his decision
came quickly.

"Can you get us an iron bar, or a pick, . . . something to make
a hole in the wall?"

"Sure, whatever you need, . . . but . . ."

"But what? . . . Where are they?"

"Well, the tools are right there, but all these houses belong to the
patrón, and I don't . . ."

Demetrio, without hearing him out, headed straight for the room
where he'd been told the tools were stored.

In a matter of minutes they had dug through the wall.

As soon as they were in the alley, one after another, staying close
to the wall, they ran forward until they were in position behind the
temple.

First they had to jump over one wall, and then the high wall behind the chapel.

"This is God's work we're doing," thought Demetrio. And he was the first one over.

Like monkeys, the others followed him, pulling themselves up with hands streaked with dirt and blood. The rest was easier: footholds carved into the masonry made it easy for them to scale the chapel wall; then the cupola itself shielded them from the soldiers' sight.

"Hold up for a bit," said the villager; "I'll go see where my brother is stationed. I'll signal to them . . . then we'll all open fire on the officers, eh?"

But no one paid any attention to him.

For a moment Demetrio contemplated the soldiers' black capes all along the wall in front and on both sides, at the men crowded behind the iron railing on the towers.

He smiled with satisfaction, and, turning back toward his men, shouted:

"Now!"

Twenty bombs went off simultaneously in the midst of the federal soldiers, who jumped to their feet, their eyes wide with fear. But before they fully comprehended the danger, twenty more bombs exploded with a roar, leaving a trail of dead and wounded.

"Not yet! . . . Not yet! . . . I still don't see my brother . . ." implored the villager desperately.

An old sergeant stands cursing and haranguing the soldiers, in the vain hope of getting them to regroup. But they're no more than rats scrambling in a trap. Some of the soldiers run for the little door to the stairs and fall there, riddled with bullets from Demetrio's rifle; others throw themselves at the feet of that squad of spectres whose heads and chests are as dark as iron, whose ragged white trousers go all the way down to their huaraches. In the bell tower a few men are struggling to extricate themselves from the arms and legs of the dead who've fallen on top of them.

"My *jefe*!" exclaims Luis Cervantes in alarm. "We're out of bombs, and the rifles are in the corral! What a mess!"

Demetrio smiles, pulls out a long, gleaming blade. Instantly, knives flash in the hands of his twenty soldiers; some are long and sharp, others as broad as the palm of a hand, many as heavy as axes.

"The spy!" cries Luis Cervantes in a triumphant voice. "Didn't I tell you!"

"Don't kill me, chief!" implores the old sergeant throwing himself at the feet of Demetrio, who has his knife raised to strike.

The old Indian lifts his wrinkled face, not a gray hair on his head. Demetrio recognizes the man who deceived them the previous evening.

With a horrified expression, Luis Cervantes quickly turns his face away. The steel blade bites into the ribs, which crack loudly, and the old Indian falls on his back, arms spread wide, his eyes filled with terror.

"Not my brother, no! . . . Don't kill him, he's my brother!" screams the villager, crazed with fear on seeing Pancracio throw himself on a soldier.

It's too late. Pancracio, with a single slice, has cut through his throat; two crimson streams spurt out as from a fountain.

"Kill the soldiers! . . . Kill the reactionaries!"

Pancracio and Manteca distinguish themselves in the massacre, killing off the wounded. Montañés lets his hand fall, weary now, his impassive face as gentle as ever, shining as innocently as a child's, with the amorality of a jackal.

"That one's still alive!" shouts Quail.

Pancracio runs toward him. It's the pretty blond captain with the fancy mustache, his face white as wax. He's huddled in a corner beside the spiral staircase, too weak to climb down.

Pancracio shoves him to the edge of the parapet—a knee jammed violently into his hips, and then a sound like a sack of stones falling sixty feet onto the atrium of the church.

"What a blockhead!" exclaims Quail. "If I'd guessed what you were up to, . . . I don't have to say it. Those were fine shoes, and I already had my eye on them!"

The men are busy now, stooping down to strip those with the best clothes. Trying on their spoils, they joke around and laugh, enjoying themselves immensely.

Demetrio, brushing back the long sweat-soaked locks that have fallen over his eyes and forehead, says:

"Now let's go get those rich bastards, those *curros*!"

XVIII

Demetrio reached Fresnillo with a hundred men the same day Pánfilo Natera was starting out with his troops toward Zacatecas.

The Zacatecan general welcomed him cordially.

"I've heard good things about you and your men—and about the whippings you gave the *federales* all the way from Tepic to Durango!"

Natera gripped Macías's hand effusively as Luis Cervantes pontificated, "With leaders like General Natera and my Colonel Macías, our country has a glorious future!"

Demetrio understood the purpose of those words after he had heard Natera refer to him a number of times as "my Colonel."

The wine and beer flowed freely. Demetrio clinked glasses several times with Natera. Luis Cervantes made a toast "to the triumph of our cause, which is the sublime triumph of justice; may we soon see the realization of the ideals of redemption of this noble and long-suffering land of ours, and may those who have nourished the land with their own blood reap the fruits which are theirs by right."

Natera turned his harsh gaze for an instant toward the long-winded *curro* and then, turning his back on him, started talking with Demetrio.

For some time, one of Natera's officers had been staring insistently at Luis Cervantes. He was young, with a sincere, friendly face.

"Luis Cervantes? . . ."

"Solís?"

"As soon as you came in I thought I recognized you. . . . And, what do you know! Now that I see you I can hardly believe it."

"But it's true . . ."

"So you're . . . ? But let's have a drink; come on . . ."

Solís motioned Luis Cervantes to take a seat and then started up again. "Hmmph! So since when are you a revolutionary?"

"For the past two months."

"Ah, so there's a good reason why you still speak with that enthusiasm and faith all of us had in the beginning!"

"You've lost yours?"

"Look, friend, don't be shocked at my coming right out and confiding in you so openly. It's so hard to find anyone intelligent to talk to around here that when one comes along you latch on to him as desperately as you do a glass of cold water after walking with your mouth dry for hours and hours under a hot sun. . . . But frankly, I really need for you to explain something to me before. . . . I can't understand how a reporter for *El País* during Madero's presidency, the guy who wrote such scathing articles in *El Regional,* the guy who referred to us so frequently with the epithet of 'bandits,' could suddenly have joined our ranks."

"The truth of the matter is, they've got me convinced," replied Cervantes emphatically.

"Convinced?"

Solís let out a sigh; he filled their glasses and they drank.

"So you've grown weary of the revolution?" asked Luis Cervantes guardedly.

"Weary? . . . I'm twenty-five years old and, as you can see, I'm quite healthy. . . . Disillusioned? Perhaps."

"You must have your reasons."

"'I expected a field of flowers at the end of the road . . . and I found a swamp.' My friend: there are deeds and there are men who are nothing but bile. . . . And that bile starts falling drop by drop into your soul, turning everything bitter, poisoning everything. Enthusiasm, hopes, ideals, joys . . . nothing! Then there's nothing left: either you become a bandit just like them, or you vanish from the scene, hiding behind the walls of a fierce and impenetrable selfishness."

For Luis Cervantes, the conversation was painful, to say the least; it hurt him to hear words so unsuited for this time and place. So in order to avoid taking a stand, he asked Solís to tell him in detail of the events which had led him to such a state of disenchantment.

"Events? . . . Trifles, little things: facial expressions unnoticed by almost everyone; a wrinkle appearing for an instant, then contracting, a gleam in someone's eyes, pursed lips; the fleeting meaning of a muttered phrase. But events, facial expressions and movements which, taken together in their logical and natural context, constitute and make up a whole race's mask, frightful and grotesque at the same time . . . the mask of a race that is utterly unredeemable!" He downed another glass of wine, paused for a long while, and then proceeded: "You must be wondering then why I still cling to the revolution. The revolution is the hurricane, and the man who surrenders to it is no longer a man, he's a poor dead leaf tossed about in the gale. . . ."

The presence of Demetrio, walking toward them, interrupted Solís. "Let's go, *curro* . . ."

Alberto Solís, speaking articulately and with deep sincerity, congratulated Demetrio effusively for his heroic feats, for his adventures, which had made him famous, well known even to the men of Villa's powerful Army of the North.

And Demetrio, charmed, listened to the account of his deeds, enhanced and so exaggerated that he himself didn't recognize them. Moreover, that rang so pleasantly in his ears that he ended up recounting them later in the same tone and even believing that that was the way they'd happened.

"What a great guy General Natera is!" observed Luis Cervantes on the way back to the inn. "Captain Solís, on the other hand . . . what a bore!"

Demetrio Macías, not listening, very happy, squeezed his arm and said in a whisper:

"I'm really a colonel now, *curro*. . . . And you, you're my secretary . . ."

Macías's men also made lots of new friends that night, and "for the pleasure of meeting you" the whiskey and *mezcal* flowed. And since people don't always get along together and at times alcohol can be a poor counselor, naturally there were some arguments; but everything was settled properly outside the cantina, the inn, or the brothel, without involving their friends.

The next morning, several people were found dead: an old prostitute had a bullet in her navel, and two of Colonel Macías's new recruits had holes in their heads. Anastasio Montañés informed his chief, who shrugged his shoulders and said:

"Too bad! . . . Well, let's get them buried . . ."

XIX

"They're coming back!" exclaimed the people of Fresnillo in terror when they found out the rebel attack on Zacatecas had failed.

The wild mob of sunburnt, grimy, almost naked men was returning. They wore straw sombreros with high, cone-shaped crowns and extremely wide brims that hid half their faces.

They called them the "high hats." And they were returning as happily as they had marched off to war a few days earlier, looting each town, each hacienda, each hamlet, and even the most wretched huts they found in their path.

"Who'll buy this machine from me?" called out one, red-faced and exhausted from the weight of the prize he'd managed to carry that far.

It was a new typewriter, which caught everyone's eye because of its gleaming nickel trim.

In a single morning the Oliver had changed hands five times. It had gone for ten pesos on the first trade, but then depreciated one or two pesos with each change of owner. The truth was, it weighed too much and no one could carry it for more than half an hour.

"I'll give you twenty-five centavos for it," offered Quail.

"It's yours," replied the owner, handing it over quickly, obviously afraid he'd change his mind.

Quail, for twenty-five centavos, had the pleasure of taking it in his hands and flinging it with all his might against the stones, where it broke apart noisily.

That was like a signal: all the men who were carrying heavy or unwieldy objects began to get rid of them, smashing them against the rocks. Items made of glass and porcelain, thick mirrors, brass candlesticks, exquisite statuettes, Chinese vases—all the useless things taken as spoils during the march—were smashed to pieces along the road.

Demetrio, who took no part in that merriment, so totally inappropriate considering the outcome of the military operation, called Montañés and Pancracio to one side and said to them:

"These guys are gutless. It's not that hard to capture a town. Look, first you spread out like this . . . then you concentrate your forces, you keep building up force until . . . Zap! . . . And it's over!"

And he opened his powerful, sinewy arms in a sweeping gesture;

then he brought them together gradually as though to illustrate his words until he pressed them tightly against his chest.

Anastasio and Pancracio found this explanation so simple, clear and convincing that they answered, "That's the God's truth! . . . Those guys are gutless!"

Demetrio's men set up quarters in a corral.

"Do you remember Camila, *compadre* Anastasio?" sighed Demetrio, stretched out on his back on a pile of manure, where all of the men, settled in now, were yawning with weariness.

"Who's this Camila, *compadre*?"

"The girl who brought my food to me, back there in that little hamlet."

Anastasio made a gesture as though to say: "I'm not interested in anything having to do with women."

"I can't get her out of my mind," Demetrio went on, talking with his cigarette in his mouth. "I was in bad shape. She'd just brought in a gourd filled with cool blue water. 'Don't you want some more?'– that's what the young dark-skinned girl asked me. . . . Well, I was just about knocked out from the fever, and all I could see was this gourd of blue water and then her soft voice: 'Don't you want some more?'. . . But a voice, *compadre,* that sounded as sweet in my ears as one of those little silver street organs. . . . Hey, what do you say, Pancracio, want to go back there with me?"

"Look, Demetrio, compadre, you're not going to believe me, but I've had lots of experience with women . . . Women! They're okay for a while . . . but look how it ends up! Look at me, I've got scars and scratches all over my body from messing with them! To hell with them! They're worse than the devil. Really, *compadre,* . . . but I can tell you don't believe me. But you'll find out . . . I know what I'm talking about."

"When are we going back to that *ranchito,* Pancracio?" insisted Demetrio, exhaling a puff of gray smoke.

"You just say the word. . . . You know I left my love back there too. . . ."

"Yours . . . and mine!" said Quail in a sleepy voice.

"Yours . . . and mine, too. It's nice you're so thoughtful, going off like this to bring our sweetheart back," teased Manteca.

"Yeah, man! Pancracio, bring one-eyed María Antonia back with you . . . it's getting cold around here!" shouted Meco from a distance.

And everyone broke out laughing, while Manteca and Pancracio started up a new round of insults and obscenities.

XX

"Villa's coming!"

The word spread like lightning. "Ah, Villa!" The magic word. The very image of the Great Man—the invincible warrior who exerts even at a distance the hypnotic power of a boa constrictor.

"Our Mexican Napoleon!" exclaimed Luis Cervantes.

"Yes, 'the Aztec Eagle who has buried his iron beak in the head of the serpent, Victoriano Huerta,' . . . as I said in a speech I gave in Ciudad Juárez." General Natera's adjutant, Alberto Solís, spoke in a somewhat ironic tone.

The two of them, sitting at the bar of a cantina, were downing glasses of beer.

And the rebels in their high-peaked sombreros, woolen scarves around their necks, heavy high-top shoes made of soft cowhide, their hands calloused like those of a cowboy, eating and drinking incessantly, spoke only of Villa and his troops.

Macías's men listened with their mouths open wide in astonishment at the stories Natera's men were telling:

"Oh, Villa! . . . The battles of Ciudad Juárez, Tierra Blanca, Chihuahua, Torreón!"

Just seeing and experiencing the events didn't mean much. You had to hear the stories of their portentous deeds, where right after the description of a surprisingly magnanimous deed would come the meanest and most bestial act. Villa is the invincible lord of the sierra, the eternal victim of all governments, who pursue him like a wild beast. Villa is the reincarnation of the ancient legend: the bandit named Providence who goes through the world carrying the luminous torch of an ideal: stealing from the rich to give to the poor! And the poor shape a legend around him that time will embellish so it can live on generation after generation.

"But one thing I can tell you, friend Montañés," said one of Na-

tera's men. "If General Villa takes a shine to you, he'll give you a hacienda, a whole ranch; but if you cross him . . . he'll have you shot
on the spot!"

Ah, and the men who rode with Villa! All northerners, all handsome, with Texas sombreros, brand new khaki uniforms and four-
dollar shoes from the United States.

And when Natera's men said this, they looked at each other sadly,
fully aware of the condition of their own huge straw sombreros rotted by the sun and sweat, the ragged shirts and trousers that only
half covered their filthy, louse-infested bodies.

"Because up there no one's ever hungry. . . . They've got freight
cars filled with oxen, sheep and cows, carloads of clothes, whole train-
loads of artillery and armaments, enough food so you can burst eating
if you want."

Then they started talking about Villa's airplanes.

"Ah, the airplanes! Here on the ground, close up, you don't know
what they are; they look like canoes, or small barges; but when they
start to take off, friend, the noise makes you dizzy. Then it's like an
automobile moving at full speed. Or imagine a huge bird, enormous,
which suddenly seems as if it's not even moving. And here's the really
good part: inside that bird, some gringo's got thousands of hand
grenades! Imagine what that would be like! When it's time for the
battle, just like someone tossing grain out for the hens, there go
handfuls and handfuls of lead for the enemy. . . . And the battle-
field turns into a cemetery: corpses here, corpses there, corpses all
over the place!"

And when Anastasio Montañés asked the guy if Natera's men had
fought side by side with Villa, they suddenly realized that everything
they were talking about so enthusiastically was just stuff they'd heard,
because none of them had ever seen Villa face to face.

"Hmm . . . well, it seems to me that man for man we're all
equal! . . . And what I really think is, no one's any more of a man
than anyone else. To fight, all you need is just a little pride. Me? Who
would have expected me to be a soldier or anything else! But, listen, no matter how bedraggled I look . . . I bet you don't believe
me! . . . Hey, but really, I don't have to be doing this. . . ."

"I've got my twenty head of oxen! . . . I bet you don't believe me!" said Quail behind Anastasio's back, imitating him and laughing loudly.

XXI

The thunder of the artillery diminished and sounded more distant. Luis Cervantes got up the nerve to stick his head out of his hiding place in the ruins of some fortifications at the top of the hill.

He hardly knew how he had gotten there. He didn't know when Demetrio and his men had disappeared from his side. Suddenly he was all alone, and then, caught up in an avalanche of infantrymen, he was thrown from the saddle; after being trampled to the ground, he struggled to his feet and someone on horseback had reached down and hoisted him up. Moments later the horse and both riders were knocked to the ground, and the next thing he knew he was lying in a hole, no rifle, no pistol, no nothing, surrounded by that pile of broken adobe which had provided him sanctuary, bullets whistling overhead, a pall of white smoke blanketing the hill.

"*Compañero!*"

"*Compañero!*"

"My horse threw me and they were all over me; they thought I was dead, so they took my weapons. . . . What could I have done?" explained Luis Cervantes, feeling guilty.

"No one knocked me off my horse . . . I'm here to save my hide, you know what I mean?"

The mocking tone of Alberto Solís's voice made Luis Cervantes blush. "Christ," exclaimed the former. "What a tiger that chief of yours is! Such daring, such poise! It's not just me, even the toughened veterans were standing there with their mouths open."

Luis Cervantes, embarrassed, didn't know what to say.

"Ah! You weren't there? Good for you! You found a safe place just in time! . . . Look, friend, come with me, I'll tell you all about it. Let's go over there, behind that rock. See how on that side, at the foot of that hill, there's no way in except right where we're standing; to the right the path is too steep, so it's impossible to maneuver there; it's just about as bad on the left: there the slope is so dangerous, you take one false step and you'll fall over the edge and be torn to pieces on the sharp edges of those rocks. Well, then, half of us in Moya's brigade were spread along the slope, dug in, ready to start the assault against the first line of trenches of the *federales*. The bullets were whistling over our heads; there was fighting everywhere; then, for a moment, they stopped firing on us. We assumed they were under heavy attack from the rear, so we charged the trenches. Ah, my friend, try to imagine what happened to us! . . . Halfway down the slope, there's a veritable carpet of dead bodies. The machine guns are what did it; they literally swept us away; only a few of us made it back. The generals were livid, trying to make up their minds if they dared order a new charge with the reinforcements that had only just arrived. That was when Demetrio Macías, without waiting or asking for orders from anyone, cried out, '*Arriba, muchachos!*' 'You're out of your mind!' I shouted, amazed. The officers, caught by surprise, didn't say a thing. Macías's horse, as if it had eagle's claws instead of hoofs, scrambled up these rocks. His men were screaming, '*Arriba, arriba!*' and following right on his heels like deer scrambling over the rocks, men and horses fused into one. Only one boy lost his footing and tumbled over the edge; the rest were over the crest in no time, storming the trenches and slashing the soldiers with their knives. Demetrio lassoed the machine guns, pulling on them as if they were wild bulls. That couldn't continue. The numerical disadvantage would have meant their annihilation in less time than it took them to get up there. But we took advantage of the enemy's momentary confusion and charged their positions with dizzying speed, routing them easily. Ah, what a fine soldier your chief is!"

From the top of the hill they could see one side of Bufa peak, its topmost crag shaped like the feathered head of some proud Aztec king. The slope, nearly six hundred meters long, was covered with corpses, their hair tangled, their clothes stained with mud and blood, and among those piles of warm bodies, women dressed in rags were trotting back and forth like hungry coyotes, turning the bodies this way and that, looking for spoils.

Amid the white smoke from the artillery and the black clouds coming from the burning buildings, a few houses with wide doors and multiple windows, shut tight, were shining in the sun; the streets seemed to pile up on each other, to wind back on themselves and intertwine in picturesque layers, as if they were trying to scale the surrounding hills. And above those cheerful houses rose the slender columns of a warehouse and the towers and cupolas of the churches.

"How beautiful the revolution is, even in its savagery!" proclaimed Solís with emotion. Then, suddenly melancholy, he said in a low voice:

"A pity that what's coming next won't be so beautiful. We won't have long to wait. Just until there are no more combatants, until the only gunfire you hear is that coming from the mobs indulging themselves in the pleasures of pillaging; until the psychology of our race shines forth in resplendent clarity, like a drop of water, condensed in two words: *rob* and *kill*. . . . How frustrating it would be if we who've come to offer all our enthusiasm, our very lives to overthrow a murderous tyrant, turned out to be the architects of a pedestal enormous enough to hold a couple hundred thousand monsters of the same species! . . . A people without ideals, a land of tyrants! . . . All that blood shed in vain!"

Large numbers of federal soldiers were struggling up the slope pursued by rebel troops with their huge straw sombreros and their loose-fitting white trousers.

A bullet whistled by.

Albert Solís, standing with his arms crossed, deep in thought after his last words, looked up in alarm and said:

"*Compañero,* damned if I like these buzzing mosquitoes. Let's move away from here!"

Luis Cervantes's smile was so full of scorn that Solís, embarrassed, calmly sat down on a rock.

His smile faded again as he watched the smoke wafting up from the rifles and the clouds of dust rising from each house or roof that collapsed. And he thought that he'd discovered a symbol of the revolution in those clouds of smoke and in those clouds of dust rising together so fraternally, embracing, merging together and then vanishing into nothingness.

"Ah," he cried suddenly, "now I understand!"

And his outstretched hand pointed to the railroad station. The trains chugging furiously, throwing up thick columns of smoke, the coaches crowded with people escaping at full steam.

He felt a dull thud in his stomach, and as if his legs had suddenly turned to putty, he slid off the rock. A moment later his ears began to buzz. . . . Then, eternal darkness and silence . . .

Second Part

I

Demetrio Macías prefers the limpid Jalisco tequila to the champagne where the candlelight is dissipated in the shimmering bubbles.

Dozens of filthy, ragged men are crowded around the tables of a restaurant, their skin caked with dirt, smoke, and sweat, their beards and hair matted and unkempt.

"I killed two colonels," roars a short, fat man in a harsh, guttural voice. He's wearing a braided sombrero, a chamois jacket, and a bright purple silk scarf around his neck. "They were too fat to run! You should have seen them tripping over stones, trying to make it up the hill; their faces were red as tomatoes, tongues down to their knees! . . . 'Don't run so hard, you reactionary bastards,' I yelled; 'Stop, I don't like frightened hens. . . . Stop, you bald-headed pigs, I'm not going to hurt you! Trust me!' Ha! Ha! Ha! . . . The stupid fuckers bought it! *Pow! Pow!* Just one shot each . . . then they got their rest!"

"I let one of those snooty bastards get away," said a soldier with a swarthy face, seated in one corner of the saloon, between the wall and the bar, his rifle propped between his legs stretched out in front of him. "Ah, the son of a bitch had gold braid all over his uniform! I nearly went blind looking at all the gold and silver galloons on his epaulets and even on his saddle blanket! And what did I do? . . . Ass that I am, I just watched him go by. He even pulled out his handkerchief and waved it at me, and I just stood there with my mouth open. I barely had time to take cover, when he starts blasting away at me! . . . I let him empty his magazine, and then I shouted, 'Now it's my turn!' . . . Sweet Mother of Jalpa, I didn't like that son of a ————! Then he put the spurs to his horse. . . . What a horse! Sailed right over my head, quick as lightning! . . . But another poor sucker who was coming along the same street paid the price. . . . Him I strung out to dry!"

The words come streaming out of their mouths, and as they get caught up in the account of their adventures, women with dark olive complexions, bright eyes, and flashing teeth, revolvers strapped to their waists, full cartridge belts slung across their chests, and wearing large straw sombreros, move from group to group like stray dogs. A girl with extremely coarse features and dark bare arms, her cheeks painted bright red with rouge, hops onto the bar of the cantina, right beside Demetrio's table.

He turns his face toward her and is met by a pair of lascivious eyes peering out from beneath a low forehead with thick hair parted down the middle.

The door bursts open, and in come Anastasio Montañés, Pancracio, Quail, and Meco, their mouths wide open in amazement.

Anastasio shouts in surprise and hurries over to greet the short, fat *charro* with the fancy braided sombrero and purple scarf.

They're old friends who recognize each other now after a long separation and embrace so tightly their faces turn black.

"Demetrio, compadre, let me introduce you to *el güero,* or Margarito as he calls himself. A real friend! . . . Ah, how I love this rascal! You'll see what I mean, *compadre* . . . He's all right! . . . Hey, Güero, you remember Escobedo Prison, back there in Jalisco? A whole year we spent together!"

Demetrio, who had kept silent and aloof amid the general uproar, held out his hand and mumbled with the cigar still in his mouth:

"Glad to meet you . . ."

"So you're Demetrio Macías?" interjected the girl on the bar, swinging her legs back and forth and brushing her leather shoes against Demetrio's back.

"At your service," he answered, barely turning his face.

Indifferently, she kept swinging her legs, showing off her blue stockings and the bare skin showing above them.

"Hey, Pintada! . . . what are you doing here? . . . Come on, hop down, I'll buy you a drink," said the light-skinned Margarito.

The girl accepted his offer without hesitation and boldly pushed her way through the crowd and took a seat across from Demetrio.

"So you're the famous Demetrio Macías, the hero of Zacatecas?" she asked.

Demetrio nodded his head, while *el güero* Margarito exploded into laughter, saying:

"Damn if you're not a sly one, Pintada! . . . You're going to break in a general!"

Demetrio, oblivious to what was going on, raised his eyes toward her; they stared at each other eye to eye like two strange dogs sniffing at each other suspiciously. But Demetrio couldn't withstand the girl's furiously provocative look and he lowered his eyes.

Some of Natera's officers, from their seats, began to joke around, making obscene remarks directed at La Pintada. But she wasn't flustered. "My General Natera's going to pin a little eagle on you. . . . Here, let's shake on it!"

And she held her hand out toward Demetrio and gave him a man's handshake.

Demetrio, puffed up by all the congratulations that were raining down on him, ordered a round of champagne.

"No, I don't want any wine right now, I don't feel so good," said the light-skinned Margarito to the waiter; just bring me some ice water."

"I want something to eat, as long as it isn't chili with beans—whatever you've got." ordered Pancracio.

Officers kept coming in, and pretty soon the restaurant was full. Stars and insignia of every shape and color were pinned to their sombreros; they wore large silk bandanas around their necks, diamond rings on their fingers, and heavy gold watch chains hanging down from their breast pockets.

"Hey, waiter," shouted *el güero* Margarito, "I ordered ice water. . . . I'm not asking for charity, you know what I mean? . . . See this wad of bills? . . . I could buy you . . . and your old lady thrown in, get it? I don't care if they've run out or why they've run out . . . I'm sure you know where you can get me some. . . . Look, you don't want to get me mad! I want ice water, not explanations. . . . You bringing it or not? . . . Oh, you're not? . . . Then take this . . ."

The waiter crumples under the force of a tremendous slap in the face.

"That's how I am, General Macías, my friend; look, there's not a hair left on my face, and do you know why? Because I get pissed, and when I don't have anyone around to take it out on, I start yanking out my hair until I calm down. Word of honor, General! If I didn't do that, I'd die of pure rage!"

"Yeah, it's real bad to have to swallow your own bile," chimes in very seriously a guy wearing a sombrero big enough to cover a shack. "Back there in Torreón, I killed a woman who wouldn't sell me a plate of enchiladas. They were someone else's. I didn't get what I wanted, but at least I didn't take any crap."

"I killed a shopkeeper in the town of Parral because when he gave me change, two of the bills had Huerta's picture on them," bragged another guy, who was wearing a little star, diamond rings flashing on his filthy, calloused fingers.

"Hey, in Chihuahua I killed a dude because every time I went in to this place to have lunch, he was always sitting at the same table at the same time of day. . . . That really got to me! . . . What else could I do?"

"Well, listen to this. I killed . . ."

The theme is inexhaustible.

In the early hours of the morning, when the restaurant is jumping with fun and the floor is covered with spit, when heavily made-up young women from the outskirts have begun to mingle with the dusky, dark-faced women from the north, Demetrio takes out his chiming gold watch inlaid with gaudy stones and asks Anastasio Montañés what time it is.

Anastasio looks at the watch face, then he sticks his head out a window and, looking at the starry sky, says:

"The Pleiades are sinking below the horizon, *compadre;* the sun will be up soon."

Outside the restaurant, drunken men are still shouting, laughing and singing. Soldiers gallop by, pounding the sidewalks. Pistols and rifles are going off all over the city.

And down the middle of the street, Demetrio and La Pintada are reeling, arms around each other's waist, heading for the hotel.

II

"How dumb can you be!" exclaimed La Pintada, roaring with laughter. "What planet are you guys from? Don't you know soldiers don't have to stay in hotels anymore? Really, where did you come from? You just go up to the first house you see that suits your fancy and take it. You don't ask anyone's permission! Otherwise, what was the revolution for? For the fat cats? Hell no, now we're the fat cats! . . . Hey, Pancracio, lend me your bayonet. . . . Rich sons of bitches! . . . They keep everything under lock and key."

She jammed the steel point into the crack of a drawer and, using the handle as a lever, broke open the lock and lifted the splintered desk top.

Anastasio Montañés and Pancracio and La Pintada sank their hands into the pile of letters, pictures, photographs and papers scattered on the carpet.

Pancracio showed his anger at not finding anything he liked by kicking a framed picture into the air with the toe of his sandal; the glass shattered against the candelabrum hanging in the center of the room.

They pulled their empty hands away from the pile of papers, mouthing obscenities.

But La Pintada, tireless, kept breaking open drawer after drawer, until there wasn't a nook or cranny anywhere that she hadn't searched.

They didn't notice a small jewel box lined in gray velvet that fell and rolled silently along the floor to where Luis Cervantes was standing. He looked around with an air of profound indifference. There was Demetrio, sprawled on a rug, seemingly asleep. Luis moved the little box toward himself with the toe of his shoe; he stooped down, scratched his ankle, and palmed the box deftly.

He was stunned: two crystal clear diamonds set in silver filigree. He hastily slipped the box into his pocket.

When Demetrio awoke, Luis Cervantes said to him:

"General, look what a mess the men have made. Shouldn't we stop them from behaving like that?"

"No, *curro*. . . . Poor wretches! . . . That's the only pleasure they have left after offering their bellies up for target practice."

"Yes, General, but they shouldn't be doing it here. . . . Look, this hurts our prestige, and what's worse, it hurts our cause. . . ."

Demetrio fixed his eagle eyes on Luis Cervantes. He drummed two fingernails against his teeth and said:

"Don't blush, now. . . . Look, you don't have to make excuses! . . . We agree, what's yours is yours and what's mine is mine.

You got yourself a little box, fine; me, I got a gold watch that chimes on the hour."

And now the two of them, in mutual agreement, showed off their booty to each other.

Meanwhile, La Pintada and her pals were searching the rest of the house.

Quail came walking in followed by a little twelve-year-old girl, who already had brown bruises on her forehead and arms. They stopped short and stood contemplating in amazement the books piled in heaps on the rug, tables and chairs, heavy mirrors smashed against the floor, large framed prints and portraits destroyed, broken furniture and bric-a-brac scattered about the room. With greedy eyes, scarcely breathing, Quail started digging for booty.

Outside, in one corner of the patio, dense smoke rising around him, Manteca stood boiling ears of corn, keeping the fire blazing with books and papers he tossed onto the coals.

"Hey!" shouted Quail. "Look what I found! These great sweat-blankets for my mare!"

And with a powerful tug he tore down a felt curtain, which fell, rod and all, onto the finely carved back of an elegant armchair.

"Wow! . . . Look at all these naked women!" shrieked Quail's little girl, highly amused by the illustrations of a luxury edition of the *Divine Comedy*. "I really like this, and I'm keeping it."

And she began tearing out the pictures that appealed to her most. Demetrio pulled himself up and sat down next to Luis Cervantes. He ordered a beer and held out a bottle to his secretary, downing his in a single gulp. Then, drowsy, he half closed his eyes and went back to sleep.

"Hey," a man called to Pancracio from the doorway, "when do I get to talk to your general?"

"You don't get to talk to him at all. He woke up with a hangover." answered Pancracio. "What do you want?"

"I want him to sell me some of those books they're burning."

"I'll sell them to you."

"For how much?"

Pancracio, perplexed, squinched up his eyebrows: "For the ones with pictures, five cents apiece, and the others . . . I'll throw them in if you buy the whole pack."

The man came back in with a basket for the books.

"Demetrio, hey, Demetrio, come on, wake up!" shouted La Pintada. "Don't just lie there sleeping like a fat pig! Look who's here! . . . It's Güero, you know, . . . Margarito! This Güero is a hell of a guy, in case you didn't know."

"I have a lot of respect for you, General Macías, and I've come here to tell you how much I like you and your way of doing things. So, if you don't have any objections, I'd like to join your brigade."

"What's your rank?" asked Demetrio.

"I'm a captain, General."

"Fine, join us then. Now you're a major."

El güero Margarito was a short fat little man with a waxed mustache. When he laughed, his shifty blue eyes disappeared between his fat cheeks and his forehead. An ex-waiter at the Delmonico in Chihuahua, now he swaggered around with three brass bars to indicate his rank in the Northern Division.

Güero heaped praise on Demetrio and his men, and that was all it took for a case of beer to be finished off in short order.

La Pintada suddenly appeared in the middle of the room, strutting around in a splendid silk dress with exquisite lace trim.

"All that's missing are the stockings!" exclaimed the light-skinned Margarito, cracking up with laughter.

Quail's girl burst out laughing too.

But La Pintada wasn't fazed; she shrugged her shoulders indifferently, threw herself down on the rug, kicked off her white linen shoes, happily wiggling her bare toes which were stiff from the tight shoes, and said: "Hey, you, Pancracio! . . . Go get me some blue stockings from my take."

The room was filling up with new friends and old companions from the campaign. Demetrio, with renewed energy, began to relate in detail some of his more notable exploits.

"But, what's that noise?" he asked, startled by the tuning up of string and brass instruments out in the patio.

"General," said Luis Cervantes solemnly, "it's a banquet your

old friends and companions are throwing for you in order to cele-
brate the victory at Zacatecas and your well-deserved promotion to
general."

III

"General Macías, may I introduce my future wife to you," said Luis
Cervantes emphatically, as he led a girl of rare beauty into the dining
room.

Everyone turned to look at her as her big blue eyes opened wide
with wonder.

She was barely fourteen, with skin as pink and smooth as a rose
petal; she had blond hair, and the childlike fear in her eyes had just
a touch of mischievous curiosity.

Luis Cervantes observed that Demetrio was staring at her with
predatory eyes, and he felt pleased.

They made a place for her between *el güero* Margarito and Luis Cervantes, right across from Demetrio.

A great many bottles of tequila stood among the cut-glass bowls,
the porcelain dishes, and the flower vases.

Meco came in cursing and sweating, with a box of beer on one
shoulder.

"You guys don't really know my friend Güero yet," said La Pintada, noticing how he couldn't take his eyes off Luis Cervantes's fiancée.
"He's got spirit, and I've never met a guy with more style."

She gazed at him lecherously and added: "That's why I can't stand
him!"

The orchestra broke into a loud bullfight march.

The soldiers roared with happiness.

"What fine tripe, General! . . . I swear I've never tasted any better," said *el güero* Margarito, and he started reminiscing about the
Delmonico in Chihuahua.

"Do you really like it, Güero?" asked Demetrio. "Well, have them
keep filling your bowl until you're stuffed."

"It's exactly the way I like it," Anastasio Montañés chimed in, "and
here's the best part: when I like something, I eat and eat until I belch."

Then came the sound of mouths slurping and throats gulping. Everyone drank copiously.

Finally, Luis Cervantes stood up with a glass of champagne in his hand: "General . . ."

"Hmmph!" interrupted La Pintada. "Here comes a speech, and that's something that bores the hell out of me. I think I'll go out to the corral, since there's nothing left to eat anyway."

Luis Cervantes held out the black cloth shield on which was pinned a small brass eagle, offering a toast which no one understood but which they nonetheless applauded noisily.

Demetrio took the insignia of his new rank in his hands and, all excited, with his eyes bright and his teeth shining, said with great simplicity: "What am I supposed to do with this buzzard?"

"Brother," said Anastasio Montañés in a trembling voice, still standing, "I don't have to tell you . . ."

Whole minutes went by; the accursed words Anastasio wanted to pronounce wouldn't come forth. His red face and forehead were beaded with sweat and streaked with grime. Finally he managed to complete his toast:

"Well, I don't have to tell you . . . except that you already know I'm your pal. . . ."

And since everyone had applauded Luis Cervantes, Anastasio himself, when he finished, gave the signal, clapping very seriously.

But nobody minded, and his awkwardness acted as a stimulus. Manteca and Quail both offered toasts.

As Meco started to give a toast of his own, La Pintada came running in, screaming for joy. Clicking her tongue, she was trying to lead a beautiful jet-black mare into the dining room.

"My booty! My booty!" she shouted, patting the arched neck of the proud animal.

The mare wouldn't go through the door, but a jerk on the reins and a crack of the whip across its withers made it step in with a clatter, head high.

The soldiers, amazed, contemplated the rich prize with poorly concealed envy.

"I don't know what that devil La Pintada has going for her; she always gets the best booty!" shouted *el güero* Margarito. "It's been that way ever since she joined us in Tierra Blanca."

"Hey, you, Pancracio, go get me some alfalfa for my mare," ordered La Pintada abruptly.

Then she turned the reins over to a soldier.

Once again they all filled their glasses and cups. A few men started to let their heads fall forward and their eyes droop, but most of them were shouting jubilantly.

And among them Luis Cervantes's sweetheart, who had spilled all her wine on her handkerchief, was turning her big blue eyes this way and that, frightened.

"Boys," shouted *el güero* Margarito, on his feet now, his shrill, guttural voice making itself heard above the tumult, "I'm tired of living, and all of a sudden I feel like killing myself. I'm fed up with La Pintada . . . and this little cherub from heaven won't even give me a tumble . . ."

Luis Cervantes was aware that these last words were addressed to his fiancée, and with great surprise he realized that the foot he had felt between the girl's legs hadn't been Demetrio's, but Güero's. He was boiling over with anger.

"Get this, boys," continued Güero, with his revolver held high over his head. "I'm going to put a bullet right in the middle of my forehead!"

And he aimed at the large mirror in the back of the room, where his whole body was reflected.

"Don't move a hair, Pintada!"

The mirror shattered into long, sharp fragments. The bullet had grazed La Pintada's hair. She hadn't even blinked.

IV

Late in the afternoon Luis Cervantes awoke, rubbed his eyes, and sat up. He was lying on the hard ground, among the large flower pots in the garden. Close by, snoring loudly, Anastasio Montañés, Pancracio, and Quail were sound asleep.

His lips were swollen and his nose felt dry and crusted with blood. There was blood on his hands and shirt, and immediately he remembered what had happened. He stood up abruptly and walked over toward a bedroom; he pushed on the door several times, but couldn't get it open. He stood there perplexed for a few seconds.

Because it was all true. He was sure he hadn't dreamed it. He had gotten up from the dining room table with his girlfriend, led her into the bedroom; but before he had closed the door, Demetrio, staggering drunk, had rushed after them. Then La Pintada followed Demetrio, and they began to struggle. Demetrio, his eyes burning like coals, with clear threads of saliva on his thick lips, was looking wildly for the girl. La Pintada, shoving him fiercely, had made him draw back.

"But, you, what! . . . What the hell are you doing!" Demetrio howled in rage.

La Pintada stuck her leg between his, used it as a lever, and Demetrio sprawled full-length, outside the room.

He got up furiously.

"Help! . . . Help! . . . He's going to kill me!"

La Pintada grabbed Demetrio's wrist and pushed aside the barrel of his pistol.

The bullet buried itself in the bricks. La Pintada continued yelling. Anastasio Montañés came up behind Demetrio and disarmed him.

Demetrio, like a bull in the middle of the ring, looked back wild-eyed. Luis Cervantes, Anastasio, Manteca, and several others had him surrounded.

"Bastards! . . . You've taken my pistol! As if I needed a fucking gun to handle punks like you!"

And flinging out his arms, in just seconds he knocked anyone he could reach sprawling to the brick pavement.

And after that? Luis Cervantes couldn't remember anything more. Undoubtedly, they'd been beaten soundly and left to sleep it off. Surely, his fiancée, frightened by so many rough men, had had the wisdom to lock herself in.

"Maybe this bedroom connects to the living room and I can get in through there," he thought.

The sound of his footsteps awakened La Pintada, who had been sleeping on the rug beside Demetrio at the foot of a love seat piled high with alfalfa and corn where the black mare had been eating.

"What are you looking for?" she asked. "Ah, sure, I know what you want! . . . Shameless bastard! . . . Look, I locked your girlfriend up because I couldn't control that damn Demetrio any longer. Take the key. It's over there on the table."

Luis Cervantes searched in vain through all the hiding places in the table.

"Tell me, *curro,* how'd you end up with that girl?"

Luis Cervantes, very nervous, kept looking for the key.

"Don't get upset, man, I'll get it for you. But tell me . . . I get a kick out of these things. That little town girl is just like you. She's not trash like us."

"I don't have anything to tell. . . . She's my fiancée, and that's it."

"Ha! Ha! Ha! Your fiancée and . . . not your ———! Look, *curro,* for every place you're going to, I've already been there! These aren't my milk teeth, you know. Manteca and Meco dragged that poor girl out of her house, that I already knew . . . but you must have bought her from them. . . . What'd she cost you, a pair of gold-plated cuff-links? . . . a picture of some miracle of the Lord Jesus of Villita? . . . Am I lying, *curro?* See, there are a few people who know what's what, but just a few! Am I right?"

La Pintada scrambled up to get the key for him, but she couldn't find it either, and she stood there perplexed.

She thought for a long while.

Suddenly she rushed out full speed toward the door of the bedroom, put one eye to the keyhole, and crouched there without moving until her vision adjusted to the darkness of the room. Then, without taking her eye away, she murmured: "Ah, Güero, . . . you son of a ———! Just take a look, *curro!*"

And she walked away, roaring with laughter.

"I tell you, in my whole life I've never seen such a guy!"

The next morning, La Pintada waited for the moment when Güero came out of the bedroom to feed his horse.

"Poor child! . . . Hurry, go home! . . . These men are capable of killing you! Get going, run!"

And over the shoulders of the little girl with the big blue eyes who looked like a virgin, and who was wearing nothing but a chemise and stockings, she lay Manteca's filthy blanket, grabbed her by the hand, and put her out in the street.

"Thank God!" she exclaimed. "Now I'll . . . how I love that Güero!"

V

Like colts neighing and frolicking at the first thunderstorm in May, Demetrio's men ride through the sierra.

"To Moyahua, boys!"

"To the land of Demetrio Macías!"

"To the land of Don Mónico, the cacique!"

The landscape brightens, the sun marks the diaphanous clarity of the sky with a scarlet streak.

Gradually the spiny vertebrae of the mountains rise into view like huge lizards; crags shaped like colossal Aztec idols, faces of giants leering out grotesquely, provoking smiles, or a vague terror, like a mysterious foreboding.

Demetrio Macías rides at the head of his men with his general staff: Colonel Anastasio Montañés, Lieutenant Colonel Pancracio, and Majors Luis Cervantes and *el güero* Margarito.

Behind them ride La Pintada and Venancio, who courts her gallantly, reciting the lovesick poetry of Antonio Plaza. As the sun's rays grazed the housetops, they rode into Moyahua four abreast, bugles sounding.

The roosters' chorus was deafening, dogs barked their alarm, but there was no sign of life anywhere from the townspeople.

La Pintada spurred her black mare forward with a leap and pulled up elbow to elbow alongside Demetrio. Very pleased with herself, she was decked out in a silk dress and heavy gold earrings. The pale blue color of the dress accentuated her olive complexion and the copper-colored blotches on her forehead and arms. She rode with her legs wide apart and her skirt hitched up to her knees, exposing the many holes in her filthy stockings. She wore a pistol across her chest and had her cartridge belt slung across the pommel of the saddle.

Demetrio was also dressed stylishly: wide-brimmed sombrero, tight leather trousers with silver buttons, and a gold-embroidered jacket.

Then came the sound of doors being kicked open. The soldiers, scattered through the town by now, were collecting weapons and saddles from every house.

"We're going to spend the morning at Don Mónico's house," said Demetrio solemnly, climbing down from his horse and handing the reins to a soldier. "We're going to have lunch with Don Mónico . . . a real good buddy of mine. . . ."

This provoked smiles and sinister laughs from his staff.

And dragging their spurs noisily along the sidewalks, they headed toward a large, ostentatious house which could only have belonged to a cacique.

"It's locked up tight," said Anastasio Montañés, pushing against the door with all his might.

"But I know how to open it," replied Pancracio, jamming his rifle against the lock.

"No, no," said Demetrio. "Knock first."

Three blows with the rifle butt. Three more, and no one answers. Pancracio takes matters into his own hands, not waiting for any more orders. He fires, the lock springs out and the door opens.

Inside, the swishing of skirts and the bare legs of children scampering toward the back rooms.

"I want wine! . . . Here, right now, wine!" demands Demetrio in a commanding voice, slamming his fist down on the table top several times.

"Sit down, *compañeros.*"

A woman appears, then another and another, and the frightened faces of children peer out from behind the black skirts. One of the women, trembling, walks toward a sideboard, takes out glasses and bottles, and serves wine.

"What kind of weapons do you have?" asks Demetrio in a harsh voice.

"Weapons?" answers the woman, her tongue limp as a rag. "What makes you think we have weapons, respectable women like us, living alone?"

"Ah, alone! . . . And Don Mónico? . . ."

"He isn't here, gentlemen. . . . We just rent the house. . . . We only know Don Mónico by name."

Demetrio orders his men to start searching the house.

"No, gentlemen, please. . . . We'll bring out everything we own, but for the love of God, don't treat us with disrespect. We're alone here, spinsters, decent women!"

"And these brats?" asks Pancracio brutally. "Did they sprout from the earth?"

The women leave the room hastily and come back moments later with an old, splintered shotgun covered with dust and cobwebs and a pistol with rusty, broken springs.

Demetrio smiles: "Okay, let's see the money . . ."

"Money? . . . But what kind of money do you expect us poor spinsters to have, living here all by ourselves?"

And they turn their imploring eyes toward the soldier standing nearest; but then their eyes narrow with horror: they've looked straight into the eyes of the Roman executioner crucifying Our Lord Jesus Christ in the *Vía Crucis* of the parish! . . . They've seen Pancracio!

Once again, Demetrio orders the search.

Together, the women rush out of the room again and come back in immediately with a moth-eaten purse. Inside are a few bills, of the kind issued by the Huerta government.

Demetrio smiles and, without any further consideration, orders his men to come in.

Like hungry dogs who have sniffed their prey, they come pouring in, knocking the women out of the way when they try to block the entrance. Some fall down in a faint, others flee; the children scream.

Pancracio is about to break the lock on a huge wardrobe when the doors open and a man leaps out with a rifle in his hands.

"Don Mónico!" they exclaim, surprised.

"Please, Demetrio! . . . Don't do anything to me! . . . Don't hurt me! . . . I'm your friend, Don Demetrio!"

Demetrio laughs sarcastically and asks him if that's the way to greet your friends, with a rifle in your hands.

Don Mónico, confused, in shock, throws himself at his feet, wraps his arms around his knees, kisses his feet: "My wife! . . . My children! . . . Please, my friend Don Demetrio!"

Demetrio, his hand shaking, puts the revolver back inside his belt. A sorrowful image has just passed through his memory: a woman with her child in her arms, trudging over the moonlit rocks of the sierra at midnight . . .

A house burning . . .

"Let's go! . . . Everyone outside!" he thunders grimly.

His staff obeys; Don Mónico and the women kiss his hands and weep with gratitude.

In the street the boisterous mob is cheerfully awaiting the general's permission to sack the cacique's house.

"I know exactly where they've hidden the money, but I'm not telling," boasts a boy with a basket under his arm.

"Hmm, I know too!" replies an old woman who's carrying a burlap sack to hold 'whatever God is pleased to provide.' "It's up on top of something; there's lots of bric-a-brac there and among it there's a small chest with shell designs. . . . That's where the good stuff is!"

"That can't be," says a man. "They're not dumb enough to leave their money lying around. The way I figure it, they've got it buried down the well in a leather bag."

And the crowd mills about, some carrying ropes to tie their bundles, others with deep wooden trays; the women spread out their aprons or the ends of their shawls, estimating how much they can carry. Everyone, giving thanks to his Divine Majesty, is waiting for a share of the plunder.

When Demetrio announces that he won't have any of that and orders everybody to move back, the townspeople obey sadly and immediately disperse; but among the soldiers there's a dull rumble of disapproval and no one moves.

Irritated, Demetrio repeats his order to disperse.

A young man, one of the new recruits who's had a bit too much whiskey, laughs and starts sauntering toward the door.

But before he can cross the threshhold, a sudden shot drops him like a bull mortally wounded by the matador's dagger.

Demetrio, unperturbed, the pistol still smoking in his hand, waits for the soldiers to move back.

"Have them set fire to the house," he orders Luis Cervantes when they reach their quarters.

And Luis Cervantes, with rare determination, without passing the order on, carries it out personally.

Two hours later, after the plaza had grown black with smoke and enormous tongues of fire were rising from Don Mónico's house, no one could explain the general's strange behavior.

VI

They had taken over a large, gloomy house, which had also belonged to the cacique of Moyahua.

The previous occupants of the estate had left their clear marks on the patio, now converted into a manure bin; on the walls, peeled and gouged with large patches of raw adobe showing through; on the floors, destroyed by the hooves of animals; and on the orchard, now a jumble of dead leaves and dry branches. Starting with the main entrance, the floor was strewn with furniture legs, the backs and seats of chairs, all covered with filth and refuse.

At ten o'clock in the evening, Luis Cervantes yawned with boredom and said goodnight to *el güero* Margarito and La Pintada, who were drinking nonstop on a bench in the square.

He walked toward the headquarters. The only room with furniture was the living room. He entered, and Demetrio, stretched out on the floor, his eyes wide open and staring at the ceiling, stopped counting the beams and turned toward him.

"Is that you, *curro*? What's up? Come on in, have a seat."

Luis Cervantes first walked over to trim the candle, then pulled over an armchair without a back, its wicker bottom now replaced with coarse hemp. The legs of the chair creaked and La Pintada's black mare snorted, moved about in the shadows, tracing a graceful curve with its round, smooth haunches.

Luis Cervantes sank down into his seat and said: "General, I've come to give my report. . . . Right here you have . . ."

"Hey, *curro* . . . I didn't want that! . . . Moyahua is like my

hometown. . . . They're going to say that's what I came here for!"
replied Demetrio, looking at the coin-stuffed sack Luis was holding
out toward him.

Luis stood up and came over to squat down beside Demetrio. He
stretched a serape out on the floor and onto it he emptied the sack
of ten-peso hidalgos. They shone like golden embers.

"In the first place, General, only you and I are going to know
about this. . . . And in the second place, you know you have to open
your window when the sun's shining. . . . Today it's shining right
in our faces, but tomorrow? . . . You have to keep looking ahead.
A bullet, a fall from your horse, even a damn cold . . . and your widow
and orphans are left in poverty! . . . The government? Ha! . . . You
go to Carranza, or Villa, or any of the important leaders and tell
them about your family; . . . if they respond with a kick in the . . . in
the you know where, tell them how good it felt. . . . And they're
right, General; we didn't go to war so some Carranza or Villa could
end up being president of the republic; we're fighting for the sacred
rights of the people, which have been trampled by the vicious cacique. . . . So since neither Villa nor Carranza nor anyone else is
going to come ask our permission to pay themselves for the services
they've been lending to the country, neither should we need to ask
anyone's permission."

Demetrio pulled himself up halfway, reached for a bottle near where
he'd been lying, drained it dry, and then, swelling his cheeks, spat
a mouthful across the room.

"You do have a way with words, *curro!*"

Luis began to feel dizzy. The spray of beer seemed to have inten-
sified the fermentation of the refuse scattered around them: a carpet
of orange and banana peels, fleshy watermelon rinds, fibrous mango
pits, and crushed sugarcane, all mixed in with the tamale cornhusks
sprinkled with chili and everything smeared with excrement.

Demetrio's calloused fingers kept running over the bright gold
coins, caressing and counting.

Recovered from his dizziness, Luis Cervantes took out a small
canister labeled Fallières Phosphate and poured out a stream of charms,
rings, pendants, and other valuable jewels.

"Look, General: if, as now seems likely, this mess is going to continue, if there's no end to this revolution, we've already got enough here to live it up for a while somewhere outside the country."

Demetrio shook his head in disapproval.

"Are you saying you wouldn't do that? . . . But why not, why should we stick around? . . . What cause are we defending now?"

"That's something I can't explain, *curro*. But I feel it's not something a man should do . . ."

"Take your pick, General," said Luis Cervantes, pointing to the row of dazzling jewels.

"You can have it all. . . . Really, *curro*, . . . try to get it through your head . . . I don't give a shit for money! . . . You want me to tell you the truth? Well, for me . . . as long as I don't run out of whiskey and I've got some sweet young girl who tickles my fancy, I'm the happiest man in the world."

"Ha! . . . What a thing to say, General. . . . Okay, if that's true, why do you put up with that snake in the grass, La Pintada?"

"Hey, *curro,* I am fed up with her. But that's how I am. I can't get up the nerve to say anything. . . . I'm not man enough to send her packing. That's me, that's how I am. Look, when I like a woman, I get tongue-tied, and if she doesn't say something, . . . I can't do a thing." And he sighed: "There's Camila, for example, the one back at the little hamlet. . . . The girl's not much to look at, but if you knew how I go for her . . ."

"You pick the day, General, and we'll bring her back here."

Demetrio winked mischievously.

"I promise I'll arrange it, General . . ."

"Really, *curro*? . . . Look, if you do that for me, this watch is yours, gold chain and all, since you like it so much."

Luis Cervantes's eyes gleamed. He picked up the phosphate canister, filled to the brim, stood up, and said with a smile: "See you tomorrow, General . . . have a good night."

VII

"What do I know? No more than you do. The general said to me: 'Quail, saddle your horse and my black mare. You're going with the *curro* on a mission.' So, that's how it was: we left here at noon and got to the hamlet just as night was falling. One-eyed María Antonia put us up. . . . She kept asking about you, Pancracio. . . . Early in the morning, the *curro* woke me up: 'Quail, Quail, saddle the horses. Leave my horse here with me and go back to Moyahua with the general's mare. I'll catch up with you in a little while.' And the sun was high in the sky when he showed up with Camila in the saddle. He helped her down, and we put her up on the black mare."

"Yeah, and what about her? How was she taking it?" asked one of the soldiers.

"Hmm, well, you couldn't get her to stop jabbering, she was so happy!"

"And what about the *curro*?"

"Quiet, just the same as always; you know how he is."

"I'll just bet," speculated Venancio very seriously, "that if Camila woke up in Demetrio's bed, it was by mistake. We had a lot to drink. . . . Think about it! . . . The alcohol went to our heads, and we all passed out."

"What alcohol? That's bullshit! . . . It was all cooked up between the *curro* and the general."

"Damn right! As far as I'm concerned, that fucking *curro* is nothing but a damn . . ."

"I don't like to talk about friends behind their backs," said *el güero* Margarito, "but I can tell you this: of the two girlfriends he's had since I've known him, one turned out to be for . . . me . . . and the other for the general!"

And they all burst out laughing.

As soon as La Pintada realized exactly what had happened, she went to console Camila, with a great show of affection.

"Poor thing, tell me what happened!"

Camila's eyes were swollen from crying.

"He lied to me, he lied to me! . . . He came to the hamlet and said to me: 'Camila, I've come back just for you. Will you come with me?' Hmmph! Can you imagine me not wanting to go away with him? Because I love him, I really love him, I really, really love him! . . . Look how thin I am from just pining over him! In the mornings I don't even feel like grinding the corn. My mama calls me

for lunch, and the tortilla sticks in my mouth . . . and such a heartache, such a heartache!"

And she began to cry again, and to keep them from hearing her
sobs she covered her mouth and nose with the end of her shawl.

"Look, honey, I'm going to get you out of this mess. Don't be
silly, now, don't cry any more. Don't think about the *curro* any
more. . . . Do you know what he is? . . . There's a name for bastards
like him! I tell you, that's all the general uses him for! . . . What a
silly thing you are! . . . Now, do you want to go back home?"

"Ay, may the Virgin of Jalpa help me! . . . My mama would beat
me to death!"

"She'll do no such thing! . . . Here, here's what we'll do. The troops
will be pulling out any time now; when Demetrio tells you to start
getting ready to leave, you tell him you're aching all over, you feel
as if someone had beat you, and you start stretching and moaning
and yawning. Then you feel your forehead and say: 'I'm burning up.'
Then I'll tell Demetrio to leave the two of us behind and that I'll
stay to take care of you and that as soon as you're better we'll catch
up with him. And what we'll do then is I'll take you back home safe
and sound."

VIII

The sun had already set, and the town lay under an oppressive
pall emanating from the dreariness of its old streets and the terrified
silence of the people, who had abandoned the streets early, when
Luis Cervantes appeared at Primitivo López's store to break up what
promised to be a first-class spree. Demetrio was getting drunk there
with his old comrades. There was no room left at the bar. Demetrio,
La Pintada, and *el güero* Margarito had tied their horses outside, but
the rest of the officers had come crashing in on their horses like savages. The enormous concave brims of their decorated sombreros
bobbed up and down constantly; the horses pranced about, turning
their fine heads this way and that, black eyes flashing, noses flaring,
delicate ears erect, punctuating the infernal din of the boisterous
drunks with snorts and the clatter of hooves and every now and then
with short, nervous neighs.

When Luis Cervantes arrived, tongues were wagging about a trivial event. A villager, with a black, bloody hole in his forehead, lay stretched out face up in the middle of the road. Opinions, divided at first, had solidified around an astute reflection made by *el güero* Margarito. That poor devil lying there dead was the church sacristan. But, the dumb shit . . . it had been all his own fault! . . . What kind of a dope goes around wearing trousers, a jacket, and a little cap? No way Pancracio's going to tolerate some dandy crossing his path!

Eight musicians playing wind instruments, faces red and round as suns, eyes bulging, and lungs straining from blasting away on their horns since early that morning, break off in the middle of a piece at Cervantes's command.

"General," he said, pushing past the men on horseback, "an urgent private message has just arrived. You've been ordered to march immediately in pursuit of Orozco's men."

The faces, clouded for a moment, brightened with joy.

"To Jalisco, boys!" shouted *el güero* Margarito, slapping the bar sharply.

"Get ready, you Guadalajara sweeties, here I come!" howled Quail, tilting back the brim of his hat.

The air reverberated with cries of rejoicing and enthusiasm. Demetrio's drinking companions, in their drunken excitement, offered to enlist in his ranks. Demetrio could barely speak, he was so happy. "Ah, let's pound those Orozquistas! . . . At last, some real men to fight! . . . No more of this picking off *federales* like rabbits or wild turkeys!"

"If I catch Pascual Orozco alive," said *el güero* Margarito, "I'll skin the soles of his feet and make him walk through the sierra for twenty-four hours . . ."

"What, is he the one who killed Señor Madero?" asked Meco.

"No," replied Güero grimly, "but he slapped my face once when I was a waiter at the Delmónico in Chihuahua."

"Saddle the black mare for Camila," Demetrio ordered Pancracio, who was already saddling his own horse.

"Camila can't go," said La Pintada quickly.

"Who asked your opinion?" replied Demetrio harshly.

"Isn't that right, Camila, that you woke up aching all over and feeling feverish?"

"Well, I . . . well, I . . . whatever Demetrio says . . ."

"Don't be stupid! . . . Tell him you can't go, tell him no . . ." whispered La Pintada in her ear anxiously.

"Well, the thing is, . . . I'm starting to like him; . . . can you believe it? . . . " answered Camila, also in a low voice.

La Pintada's face turned black with fury, and her cheeks swelled; but she didn't say anything and went over to get on the mare Güero was saddling for her.

IX

The whirlwind of dust, covering a long stretch of the road, would suddenly break into diffuse, violent masses, and then you could see the panting chests, wind-tossed manes, trembling nostrils, and wild, almond-shaped eyes, hooves extending and contracting to the rhythm of the gallop, and men with bronze faces, ivory teeth, and flashing eyes, rifles brandished aloft or slung across the saddles.

At the rear of the column, side by side, rode Demetrio and Camila; she, still trembling, her lips soft and dry; he, irritated by the futility of the day's march. Not an Orozquista in sight, not even a skirmish. A few scattered *federales,* a miserable priest with about a hundred deluded followers, all gathered under the archaic flag with the motto *Religion and Rights.* The priest was still swinging from a mezquite tree, and a number of corpses lay scattered about the field, across their chests small shields of red felt that read: *Halt! The Sacred Heart of Jesus is with me!*

"The thing is, I went ahead and collected my own salary, including back pay," said Quail, exhibiting the watches and gold rings he had taken from the priest's house.

"For this, anyone would be happy to go to war," exclaimed Manteca, swearing with every breath. "Finally a guy knows what the fuck he's risking his hide for!"

And with the same hand he used to grasp the reins, he clutched a shining ornament he'd torn from the figure of the crucified Christ in the church.

Quail, an expert in such matters, greedily examined Manteca's loot, then snorted derisively:

"Your treasure's nothing but tin!"

"Why are you bothering with that garbage?" Pancracio asked *el güero* Margarito, who, dragging a prisoner, was among the last to arrive.

"You want to know why? Because I've never seen up close the look a guy gets when you tighten a noose around his neck."

The prisoner, very fat, was gasping for breath; his face was flushed, his eyes bloodshot, and sweat was pouring down his forehead. He staggered along with his wrists and feet bound together.

"Anastasio, lend me your lasso; my halter's not strong enough for this rooster. . . . But on second thought, don't bother. . . . *Federal, amigo,* I'm going to finish you off quick, you're suffering too much. Look, those *mezquite* trees are too far away, and there's not even a telegraph pole to hang you from."

And *el güero* Margarito pulled out his pistol, jammed the barrel against the prisoner's left nipple and slowly pulled the trigger back.

The federal prisoner grew pale as a cadaver, his face tightened, and his glazed eyes began to water. His chest was heaving violently, and his whole body shivered uncontrollably.

El güero Margarito held his pistol there for what seemed an eternity of seconds. His eyes gleamed strangely, and his fat little face, cheeks puffed out, was lit up with an expression of supreme sensuality.

"No, my dear *federal,*" he said slowly, returning his weapon to its holster, "I don't want to kill you yet. . . . You're going to be my orderly. . . . You'll see what a mean son of a bitch I am!"

And he winked maliciously at those standing nearby.

The prisoner had fallen into a stupor; all he could do was to attempt to swallow; his mouth and throat were stone dry.

Camila, who had been riding in the rear, spurred her mare's flank and caught up with Demetrio:

"Ay, what an evil man that Margarito is! . . . You should see what he's doing to one of the prisoners!"

And she told what she had just seen.

Demetrio contracted his eyebrows, but gave no reply.

La Pintada called to Camila from a distance.

"Hey, you! What kind of lies are you telling Demetrio? . . . *El güero*

Margarito is my true love. . . . Just so you know! So now you know. . . . Anything you do to him, you do to me. That's your only warning!"

And Camila, very frightened, went back to Demetrio's side.

X

The men were camped on an open plain near three small houses standing side by side in that emptiness, their white walls sharply silhouetted against the purple swath of the horizon. Demetrio and Camila rode toward them.

In the corral, a man wearing a shirt and white trousers stood puffing avidly on a cornhusk cigarette; nearby another man was sitting on a slab shelling corn, rubbing the ears between his hands, one withered, twisted leg that ended in a stump like a goat's hoof constantly in motion to scare away the hens.

"Hurry up, Pifanio," said the man who was standing; "the sun's already set and you still haven't taken the animals down for water."

A horse neighed outside the corral, and the two men looked up startled.

Demetrio and Camila appeared beyond the corral fence.

"All I want is a place to sleep for me and my woman," said Demetrio, reassuring them.

And when he told them that he was the general of a small army that was camping nearby, the man who was standing, and who owned the place, invited them in with great deference. He ran to get a broom and water in a clay jug to sweep and wash the best corner of the barn to make suitable lodging for such honorable guests.

"Hey, Pifanio, get a move on; unsaddle the horses for these good people."

The man who was shelling corn pulled himself laboriously to his feet. He wore a tattered shirt and vest, ragged trousers, open at the seams, with the ends hanging loose from his waist.

He started to walk, and his forward progress traced a grotesque circle.

"But, how can you work, friend?" asked Demetrio without letting him remove the saddles.

"Poor fellow," shouted the owner from inside the barn, "he's not too strong! . . . But you should see how he earns his pay! . . . He starts working at dawn, about the time God gets up. . . . Look, the sun went down a while ago . . . and he hasn't stopped yet!"

Demetrio went out with Camila to take a turn around the encampment. The plain, its golden-brown furrows stretching endlessly into the distance, was totally bare of shrubs or grass. In that desolation, the three tall ash trees in front of the three houses, their rounded tops dark green and undulant, luxuriant branches drooping down to graze the ground, seemed almost miraculous.

"I don't know what it is about this place that makes me feel so sad!" said Demetrio.

"Yes," answered Camila, "me, too."

On the bank of a small stream, Pifanio was pulling hard on the rope of a primitive windlass. A huge clay pot was tipped over a pile of fresh grass, and in the last glimmers of afternoon light the stream of crystalline water sparkled as it poured into the trough. A skinny cow, an exhausted horse, and a burro were drinking noisily from the trough.

Demetrio recognized the crippled peasant and asked, "What do you earn per day, friend?"

"Sixteen centavos, señor . . ."

He was a tiny man with pale blue eyes, straight light-colored hair, and running sores on his neck and face. He cursed his boss, the farm, and his bitch of a life.

"You earn your salary, don't you, friend?" interrupted Demetrio gently. "You gripe and complain, but you work like hell."

And turning toward Camila: "Down here on the plains there's always someone worse off than us mountain folk, right?"

"Yes," answered Camila.

And they walked on.

The valley was shrouded in shadow and the stars hadn't yet started to peek through.

Demetrio squeezed Camila tenderly around the waist, and who knows what loving words he whispered in her ear.

"Yes," she answered faintly.

Because now she was really starting to like him.

Demetrio slept poorly, and very early in the morning he stepped out of the house.

"Something's going to happen to me," he thought.

It was a quiet, modestly cheerful morning. A thrush sang timidly in the ash tree; the animals rummaged about in the refuse in the corral; the pig grunted in his sleep. The orange flush of sunlight appeared, and the last star faded out.

Demetrio strolled slowly toward the encampment. He was thinking about his yoke of oxen—two dark beasts, almost new, barely two years working the fields—and about his two acres of rich, loamy soil. The features of his young wife were stored faithfully in his memory: those soft lines and her infinite sweetness toward her husband, her indomitable energy, and her disdain for strangers. But when he tried to reconstruct the image of his son, all of his efforts were futile; he had forgotten him.

He reached the camp. The soldiers were sleeping, sprawled out between the furrows alongside their horses, whose heads hung down, eyes closed.

"The horses are all worn out, *compadre* Anastasio; it's a good idea to stay here and rest for at least another day."

"Ay, *compadre* Demetrio! . . . How I miss the mountains! If you only knew . . . you think I'm kidding, no? . . . but I don't like anything about this place. . . . I feel so sad, so blue . . . You never know what it is that's going to make you sad!"

"How many hours from here to Limón?"

"It's not just hours: it's three hard days' riding, *compadre* Demetrio."

"You wouldn't believe how I long to see my wife!"

It didn't take La Pintada any time at all to go looking for Camila: "Tch! Tch! . . . Demetrio's going to cut you loose, just like that. He told me, told me so personally. . . . He's going to bring his real wife. . . . And she's beautiful, very fair. . . . The prettiest rosy cheeks! . . . But if you don't want to leave, maybe they can find something for you to do: they've got a child, and you can take care of it . . ."

When Demetrio returned, Camila, weeping, told him everything.

"Don't pay any attention to that bitch. . . . They're just lies, nothing but lies . . ."

And since Demetrio did not return to Limón or think any more about his wife, Camila was very happy, and La Pintada turned into a scorpion.

XI

Before dawn they set out for Tepatitlán. Spread out along the main road and fallow fields, their silhouettes swayed in rhythm with the slow, plodding movement of the horses, merging with the pearly tone of the waning moon, which cast its dim light over the whole valley.

Dogs barked in the distance.

"By noon today we'll reach Tepatitlán, then tomorrow, Cuquío, and then . . . the mountains," said Demetrio.

"Wouldn't it be a good idea, General," Luis Cervantes murmured in his ear, "to go to Aguascalientes first?"

"What for?"

"We're running out of funds . . ."

"What? . . . Forty thousand pesos in a week?"

"Just this week alone we've recruited almost five hundred men, and in advances and bonuses, it's all used up," replied Luis Cervantes very quietly.

"No. We'll head straight for the sierra. Then we'll see . . ."

"Yes, to the sierra!" several men shouted.

"To the sierra! . . . To the sierra! . . . There's nothing like the sierra!"

The flat plain continued to depress them; when they spoke of the sierra they grew enthusiastic and excited, as if it were a lover they hadn't seen for a very long time.

The day grew bright. Then, to the east, a red cloud of dust covered the sky with an immense curtain of flaming purple.

Luis Cervantes pulled back on his horse's bridle and waited for Quail.

"So where do we stand then, Quail?"

"I already told you, *curro*, two hundred for just the watch . . ."

"No, I'll buy the whole lot: watches, rings, and all the little jewels. How much?"

Quail hesitated. He turned very pale. Then he said impetuously: "Give me two thousand for everything!"

But Luis Cervantes gave himself away; his eyes gleamed with such obvious greed that Quail backed off. He exclaimed anxiously: "Hey, no, I was just fooling around; I'm not selling anything. . . . Just the watch, and only because I owe the two hundred pesos to Pancracio. He cleaned me out again last night."

Luis Cervantes pulled out four brand-new "two-faced" Villa bills and laid them in Quail's hands.

"Really," he told him, "I'm interested in the lot. . . . No one's going to give you more than I will."

When the sun began to heat up, Manteca suddenly shouted: "Hey, Güero, your orderly's trying to die on you. He says he can't walk anymore."

The prisoner had fallen down in the middle of the road, groaning from exhaustion.

"Shut up!" shouted the light-skinned Margarito, riding back toward him. "So you're already worn out, sweetheart? Aww, what a shame! I'm gonna buy you a little glass box and stick you up on a corner shelf in my house like baby Jesus. But first we have to get to town, don't we, so I'm going to help you."

And he took out his sword and whacked the poor man several times.

"Let's have that lasso, Pancracio," he said then, his eyes glowing strangely.

But when Quail pointed out to him that the *federal* wasn't moving hand or foot, he roared with laughter and said: "What a dumb shit I am! . . . And just when I'd trained him not to eat!"

"Now for sure, we're almost there, sweet little Guadalajara," said Venancio as the smiling village of Tepatitlán came into view, nestled snugly against a hill.

They entered the town in high spirits; rosy faces and lovely black eyes were shining from every window.

The schools were converted into barracks. Demetrio moved into the sacristy of an abandoned church.

Then, as usual, the soldiers spread out in search of loot, under the pretext of gathering up weapons and horses.

That afternoon, a few of Demetrio's men were sprawled about in the atrium of the church scratching their bellies. Venancio, very deliberately, his chest and back bare, was crushing the lice he found on his shirt.

A man approached the fence, requesting permission to speak to the chief.

The soldiers looked up, but no one answered him.

"I'm a widower, señores; I've got nine kids, and I can barely survive on what I make working. . . . Please don't treat us poor people so unfairly!"

"Hey, man, don't worry, we've got a woman for you," said Meco, as he smeared tallow on his feet. "We've got La Pintada there, and we'll let you have her at cost."

The man smiled bitterly.

"She's just got one bad habit," observed Pancracio, flat on his back, looking up at the blue sky; "all she has to do is see a man, and right away she juices up."

They roared with laughter; but Venancio turned serious and pointed the man toward the door to the sacristy.

The widower went in timidly and spelled out his complaint to Demetrio. The soldiers had cleaned him out. They hadn't left him even one grain of corn.

"So, why did you let them do that to you?" responded Demetrio casually.

When the man persisted, wailing and weeping, Luis Cervantes stood up, ready to throw him out rudely. But Camila intervened: "Come on, Don Demetrio, don't you be a bad guy too; tell them to give him back his corn!"

Luis Cervantes had to obey; he scrawled out a few lines, and Demetrio scratched some sort of a signature at the bottom.

"God bless you, girl! . . . God reward you with his heavenly grace. . . . Ten bushels of corn, barely enough to feed them this year," cried the man, weeping with gratitude. And he took the paper and kissed everyone's hand.

XII

They were about to enter Cuquío when Anastasio Montañés rode up to Demetrio and said:

"You know, *compadre,* I haven't told you yet . . . That *güero* Margarito's a real devil! Do you know what he did yesterday to that man who complained that we'd taken his corn for our horses? Well, the guy took the order you gave him to the barracks. 'Sure, buddy,' Güero told him, 'come on in here; it's only fair to give you back what's yours. Come in, come in. . . . How many bushels did we steal from you? . . . Ten? But are you sure it wasn't more than ten? . . . Yeah, that's more like it, say fifteen, more or less . . . or maybe it was twenty? . . . Try hard to remember. . . . You're real poor, you've got lots of kids to feed. Right, I'd say it was more like twenty; it must have been. . . . Come through here; I'm not going to give you fifteen or twenty. I'll just let you count them . . . one, two, three . . . or if you don't want to count, just tell me when to stop.' Then he took out his sword and gave him such a beating he was begging for mercy."

La Pintada was laughing so hard she nearly fell off her horse.

And Camila, unable to restrain herself, said: "What a heartless bastard he is! . . . No wonder I can't stand the sight of him!"

In a flash, La Pintada's face turned hard.

"What's it any of your business?"

Camila, frightened, spurred her mare on ahead.

La Pintada shot forward on hers and lightning-quick, bumped into Camila and, grabbing at her hair, pulled her braids loose.

At the contact, Camila's mare reared up, and the girl let go of the reins to brush the hair from her face; she swayed, then lost her balance and fell onto some rocks, splitting open her forehead.

Weeping with laughter, La Pintada, with great skill, galloped ahead to stop the runaway mare.

"Hey, *curro,* here's a job for you!" said Pancracio when he saw Camila astride Demetrio's saddle, her face covered with blood.

Luis Cervantes hurried up officiously with his first-aid kit; but Camila, stifling her sobs, dried her eyes and said in a low voice: "From you? . . . Not even if I were dying! . . . Not even a drop of water!"

There was a message waiting for Demetrio in Cuquío.

"It's back to Tepatitlán, General," said Luis Cervantes, scanning the order rapidly. "You'll have to leave the men there and go to Lagos to catch the train to Aguascalientes."

There was a heated protest: groans, complaints, and muttered oaths. Some of the men from the sierra swore they would drop out of the column.

Camila wept all night, and the next day, early in the morning, she told Demetrio she wanted permission to return home.

"Fine, if you don't like me any more! . . ." answered Demetrio sullenly.

"It's not that, Don Demetrio; I care for you . . . a lot . . . but, you've seen how it is . . . that awful woman!"

"Don't worry, I'll get her the hell out of here today. . . . I've been thinking about it."

Camila stopped crying.

Everyone was saddling up. Demetrio went over to La Pintada and told her in a very low voice, "You're not going with us."

"What do you mean?" she asked, not understanding.

"You can stay here or you can take off, wherever you want to go, but not with us."

"What are you saying?" she exclaimed in disbelief. "You mean you're giving me the boot? Ha! . . . Well, you must be some kind of fool if you believe all the lies that little ———!"

And La Pintada began to curse Camila, Demetrio, Luis Cervantes, and anyone else who came to mind with such energy and originality that the men had never even imagined such foul language before.

Demetrio waited patiently for a long while; but when she showed no signs of stopping, he said very calmly to one of the soldiers, "Throw that drunken bitch out."

"Güero, Güero, . . . Margarito, my love! Come and protect me from these . . . ! Come on, honey, show them you're a real man and they're nothing but sons of ———!"

And she flung her arms about and kicked and screamed.

El güero Margarito appeared. He had just gotten up; his blue eyes were sunken beneath swollen eyelids and his voice was raspy. He was told what was happening and, approaching La Pintada, he said to her with great solemnity: "Yeah, I think it'd be a good idea for you to clear the hell out of here . . . We're fed up with you, all of us!"

La Pintada's face turned to stone. She tried to speak, but her facial muscles were frozen.

The soldiers laughed with delight; Camila, terrified, held her breath.

La Pintada turned her eyes this way and that. Then, in an instant, it happened: she bent down, pulled out a sharp, shining blade from between her stocking and leg and threw herself on Camila.

There was a loud scream, and a body fell to the ground gushing blood.

"Kill her!" shouted Demetrio, beside himself.

Two soldiers rushed toward La Pintada, but, slashing at them with her dagger, she held them at bay.

"Not you, you bastards! . . . You kill me, Demetrio." She strode toward him, handed him her knife, thrust out her chest and let her arms fall to her side.

Demetrio raised the blood-stained dagger over his head; but his eyes clouded over, he hesitated, and then staggered back.

Then, in a choked voice, he shouted: "Get out of here! . . . Now!"

No one dared to stop her.

She walked away, without a word, grimly, one step at a time.

There was a stunned silence, broken by the sharp, guttural voice of *el güero* Margarito: "Hey, great! . . . I finally got rid of that bedbug!"

XIII

Right here in my side
he stuck his sharp knife;
he didn't know why
and neither did I . . .
Maybe he knew,
but not I . . .

Oh, how my blood gushed
from that mortal wound!
He didn't know why
and neither did I . . .
Maybe he knew,
but not I . . .

Head down, his hands crossed over the pommel, Demetrio hummed the obsessive song in a mournful tune.

Then he'd fall silent; silent and depressed for several long minutes.

"You'll see how quickly I get you out of this funk once we get to Lagos, General. There are lots of pretty girls there to cheer us up," said *el güero* Margarito.

"All I feel like doing now is getting drunk," replied Demetrio.

And he moved ahead of them once again, spurring his horse, as if he wanted to abandon himself completely to his sorrow.

After many hours of riding, he called Luis Cervantes over to him: "Listen, *curro,* now that I've had time to think about it, what the hell am I going to Aguascalientes for?"

"To cast your vote, General, for the acting president of the republic."

"Acting president? . . . Well, uh, . . . how about Carranza? . . . The truth is, I don't understand politics . . ."

They reached Lagos. *El güero* Margarito made a bet that he'd get Demetrio laughing like crazy that very night.

Dragging his spurs, his chaps fallen below his waist, Demetrio walked into "El Cosmopolita" with Luis Cervantes, *el güero* Margarito, and his orderlies.

"Why are they running, *curro?* We don't go around eating people!" exclaimed Güero.

The townspeople, caught in the act of running away, stopped short; some of them, pretending not to be frightened, went back to their tables to continue drinking and talking; others hesitantly came forward to pay their respects to the officers.

"General! . . . What a pleasure! . . . Ah, Major!"

"That's more like it! . . . That's how I like to see my friends, well-mannered and respectful!" said *el güero* Margarito.

"Come on, boys," he added, cheerfully pulling out his pistol. "Let's see you dance a little jig around this firecracker!"

A bullet ricocheted off the cement floor, passing between the table legs and the legs of the well-dressed men. They leapt up in a panic, the way a woman does when you stick a mouse under her skirt.

Pale, they smile obsequiously to ingratiate themselves with the major. Demetrio's lips barely move, but the rest of the officers roar with laughter.

"Güero," observes Quail, "that guy leaving must have been stung by that wasp. Look how he's limping."

Güero, paying no attention, and not even turning to look at the wounded man, boasts that he can draw and shoot a tequila shot glass at thirty paces.

"You, *amigo*, stop right there," he says to the boy waiting tables. Then he leads him by the hand to the entrance to the hotel patio and puts a shot glass filled with tequila on his head.

Terrified, the poor devil protests and tries to get away, but Güero pulls back the hammer on his pistol and aims. "Back to your spot, you piece of shit, or I'll pump a hot one into you for sure!"

Güero walks back to the far wall, raises his pistol, and aims.

The glass explodes, bathing the boy's deathly pale face with tequila.

"Now we'll do it for real!" he roars, running back to the bar for a new shot glass, which he places on the boy's head once again.

He goes back to his place, spins on his feet with dizzying speed, draws, and fires.

Only this time he shoots off an ear instead of the glass. And doubling over with laughter, he says to the boy: "Here, kid, take these bills. It's not serious! You can fix yourself up with a little arnica and some whiskey . . ."

After drinking a lot of alcohol and beer, Demetrio says: "Pay up, Güero. . . . I'm leaving now . . ."

"I don't have any more cash, General; but that's not a problem. . . . How much do we owe you, friend?"

"A hundred and eighty pesos, boss," responds the bartender amiably.

Güero leaps quickly over the bar, and with two sweeps of his arms he knocks over all the flasks, bottles, and glasses.

"Just send the bill to big Daddy Villa, you got it?" Staggering drunk, he accosts a very small, neatly dressed man who's closing the door to a tailor shop.

"Hey, friend, where do we go to find some girls?"

The man steps down courteously off the sidewalk to make way for him to pass. Güero stops and stares at him rudely, with real curiosity: "Say, friend, you're a pretty little thing! . . . You don't agree? . . . Are you saying I'm a liar! . . . I like that! . . . Do you know how to do the dwarf dance? . . . You don't? . . . Sure you do! . . . I saw you in a circus once! I say you're good, a first-class dancer! . . . You'll see!"

Güero pulls out his pistol and starts shooting at the tailor's feet. The tailor, a tiny fat man, gives a little hop with each shot.

"See, you really can do the dwarf dance!"

And throwing his arms over the shoulders of his friends, he has them carry him to the red-light district, marking his passage through town by spraying bullets left and right, splintering doors and walls and smashing street lights.

Demetrio leaves him and goes back to the hotel, humming to himself:

> *Right here in my side*
> *he stuck his sharp knife;*
> *he didn't know why*
> *and neither did I . . .*

XIV

Stale cigarette smoke, the pungent odor of sweaty clothes, the smell of alcohol, and the foul breath of a mob of people: the train is worse than a carload of pigs. Most of the men are wearing Texas sombreros stitched with gold braid and khaki trousers and shirts.

"Gentlemen, a well-dressed man stole my suitcase at the Silao station . . . all my savings from a lifetime of work. I've got nothing left to buy food for my child."

The voice was shrill, quavering, mournful, but it didn't carry far in the bedlam of the train coach.

"What's that old woman saying?" asked *el güero* Margarito as he came in looking for a seat.

"Something about a suitcase . . . a well-dressed child . . ." answered Pancracio, who had plopped himself down on the knees of some civilians.

Demetrio and the others were elbowing their way through the crowd, and when those suffering under Pancracio's weight decided they'd rather stand the rest of the way, Demetrio and Luis Cervantes happily squeezed into the abandoned seats.

A woman who had been standing with a child in her arms all the way from Irapuato suddenly fainted. A civilian bent down to pick up the child. The rest paid no attention: the women traveling with the troops took up two or three seats apiece with all their suitcases, dogs, cats, and parrots; the men in the Texas sombreros, on the other hand, had a good laugh at the robust thighs and soft breasts of the unconscious woman.

"Gentlemen, a well-dressed man stole my suitcase at the Silao station . . . all my savings from a lifetime of work. . . . I've got nothing left to buy food for my child!"

The old woman speaks rapidly in a singsong manner, sighing and sobbing. Her eyes, very alert, turn this way and that. She picks up a bill here, another further on. The bills begin to rain down on her. She picks them up, then moves forward a few seats:

"Gentlemen, a well-dressed man stole my suitcase at the Silao station . . ."

The effect of her words is sure and swift.

"A well-dressed man! A well-dressed man who steals a suitcase!" That's something despicable! It sparks a general feeling of outrage. What a pity that well-dressed man isn't here now so he could be shot at least once by each one of the generals traveling on the train.

"Because for me nothing's worse than a thieving *curro*!" says one, bursting with indignation.

"Robbing a poor woman!"

"Robbing a poor, helpless woman!"

And, by word and deed, they all demonstrate how tender-hearted they are: an insult for the thief and a five-peso bill for the victim.

"Let me tell you what I think: there's nothing wrong with killing, because when you kill someone it's always out of anger. But stealing, no way!" shouts *el güero* Margarito.

Everyone seems to agree with such solid reasoning. But after a brief silence and a few moments of reflection, a colonel ventures an opinion: "As a matter of fact, there's always an exception to every rule. That's a fact, and it's the truth that counts. And the pure truth is,

I myself have stolen from time to time. And if I tell you that every-one of us here has done the same, I figure that's no lie. . . ."

"Man, if you knew how many sewing machines I stole in Mexico City!" exclaimed a major vehemently, "I made more than five hun-dred pesos . . . considering I sold them for as little as fifty centavos a machine."

"Well, I stole me some real fine horses back in Zacatecas, and I said to myself: 'Pascual Mata, this is your nest egg. Now you won't have to worry about anything for the rest of your life,'" said a tooth-less old captain whose hair had already turned white. "Only trouble was, my General Limón took a fancy to my horses, and he stole them from me!"

"Okay, sure! No use denying it! I've stolen things too," *el güero* Margarito admitted. "But my comrades are here to tell you I haven't saved shit! That's for sure, because I like spending it on my friends. I'd rather get plastered with all my friends than send a centavo to the women back home. . . ."

The theme of "I stole . . . ," though it seems inexhaustible, be-gins to die out as decks of cards show up on all the seats, attracting the generals and officers like mosquitoes to light.

Soon everyone is caught up in the dramatic turns in the betting, and the atmosphere starts to heat up; it smells like a barracks, a jail, a brothel, and even a pigsty, all jumbled together.

And above the general din, in the next car, that shrill voice:

"Gentlemen, a well-dressed man stole my suitcase . . ."

The streets of Aguascalientes were now little more than a garbage dump. Like bees at the mouth of a hive, men in khaki swarmed around the doors of restaurants, run-down taverns, inns, streetstands heaped with all sorts of food, trays of rancid cracklings alongside piles of filthy cheese.

The smell of fried food stirred the appetites of Demetrio and his crew. They shoved their way in to a tavern, and a filthy, disheveled old woman brought them clay bowls of pork ribs swimming in a clear chili broth and three tough, burned tortillas. They paid two pesos apiece, and when they left, Pancracio swore he was hungrier than when he'd gone in.

"Now it's time," said Demetrio. "Let's go have that talk with General Natera."

And they went down a street toward the house where the northern general was staying.

A noisy and excited group of people blocked their way at an intersection. A man hidden by the crowd was chanting what sounded like a prayer in an unctuous, singsong voice. They moved closer until they could see him. The man, wearing a shirt and white trousers, kept repeating: "All good Catholics who say this prayer with true devotion to Christ crucified will be protected from storms, plagues, wars, and famine!"

"This guy's got it right!" said Demetrio, smiling.

The man was waving a handful of pamphlets over his head and crying: "Fifty cents for the prayer to Christ crucified, fifty cents . . ."

Then he would stoop down for a moment and pop right back up with a snake's tooth, a starfish, or a fish skeleton. And in the same pious tone he would laud the medicinal qualities and rare virtues of each object.

Quail, who had no confidence in Venancio, asked the hawker to extract a tooth for him; *el güero* Margarito purchased the black pit of a certain fruit which was supposed to immunize its owner against lightning as well as any kind of evil spell; and Anastasio Montañés bought a prayer to the crucified Christ, which he carefully folded and very reverently stuck inside his shirt.

""As sure as there's a God, *compañero,* the fight's not over! This time it's Villa against Carranza!" said Natera.

And Demetrio, saying not a word, waited wide-eyed for further explanation.

"Here's the thing," continued Natera emphatically. "The convention has refused to recognize Carranza as supreme commander and plans to elect a provisional president for the republic. . . . Do you understand, *compañero?*"

Demetrio nodded that he did.

"What do you think about that, *compañero?*" inquired Natera.

Demetrio shrugged his shoulders:

"Well, I guess it means we go on fighting. So, let's get to it. As you know, General, you can count on me."

"Fine. And who's side are you on?"

In his perplexity, Demetrio stood scratching his head for several seconds.

"Look, don't ask me any questions, I never went to school. . . . This little eagle on my hat, you're the one who gave it to me . . . so, all you have to do is tell me: 'Demetrio, do this or do that,' . . . and that's all there is to it!"

Third
Part

I

My dear Venancio,

Due to professional obligations, which take up all my time, this is the first opportunity I've had to answer your kind letter of this past January. I got my degree last December, as you know. I'm very sorry to hear about Pancracio and Manteca, though it comes as no great surprise to learn that they stabbed each other following a card game. A pity, though; they were brave guys! I deeply regret not being able to offer el güero Margarito my most heartfelt congratulations—for the noblest and most beautiful act of his life, committing suicide!

I think it's going to be very difficult here in the United States, Venancio my friend, for you to get the medical degree you so greatly desire, regardless of how much gold and silver you've accumulated in order to purchase it. I respect you, Venancio, and think you are deserving of better fortune. But you know, I've just had an idea that could be mutually beneficial and could further your admirable ambition to improve your social position. If you and I became partners, we could open a nifty business. It's true that at the moment I have no reserve funds, because I've spent everything on my studies and the graduation party; however, what I do have is something that's far more valuable than money: my perfect understanding of this town, its needs and the sure-fire commercial ventures a person can undertake. We could open an authentic Mexican restaurant, with you listed as owner, and the two of us splitting the profits at the end of each month. In addition to that, regarding something we both want: your change of social environment. As I recall, you play the guitar rather well, and I think it would be easy enough, through my recommendations and your musical talent, for you to become a member of the Salvation Army, a very respectable organization which would bestow on you considerable prestige.

Don't fiddle around, my dear Venancio. Come, bring your cash, and we'll get rich in no time. Please give my warm regards to the General, to Anastasio and our other friends.

Your true friend,
Luis Cervantes.

Venancio had just finished reading the letter for the hundredth time, and with a sigh he repeated his remark: "That *curro* knew what he was doing, all right!"

"But what I can't get through my head," observed Anastasio Montañés, "is why we have to go on fighting . . . didn't we defeat the Federation?"

Neither the general nor Venancio answered; but those words kept pounding away at their dull brains like a hammer at an anvil.

They rode pensively up the slope, heads down, swaying in rhythm with their mules' long slow strides. Anastasio, perplexed and stubborn, made the same observation to other groups of soldiers, who laughed at his naïveté. Because if you've got a rifle in your hands and plenty of shells in your cartridge belt, surely it's for the purpose of fighting. Against whom? For whom? That had never mattered to anyone!

The endless waves of dust stretched out on both sides of the trail, above a swarming anthill of straw sombreros, grimy old khakis, mildewed blankets, and the constant churning of the black horses.

The men were burning with thirst. Not a puddle nor a well nor a stream with water in it anywhere along the way. A fiery vapor rose from the white barren sides of a canyon, throbbed over the rigid tops of the *huizache* trees and the pale green, thick, flat leaves of the prickly pear plants.

And as if to mock them, the flowers opened up fresh and lush on the cactus plants, some of them fiery red, others steel-gray and diaphanous.

At midday they came upon a hut clinging to the edge of a cliff; later on, they saw three hovels stuck on the banks of a river of charred sand; but everything was silent and abandoned. Whenever the troops drew near, the people would run off and hide in the ravines.

Demetrio became angry: "Anyone you spot hiding or running away, catch them and bring them to me," he ordered his soldiers in a harsh voice.

"What do you mean? What are you saying?" exclaimed Valderrama, surprised. "These mountain folks? These courageous people who didn't run off squawking like chickens to find a safe roost in Zacatecas and

Aguascalientes? Our brothers who weather the storm clinging like moss to their rocks! I protest! . . . I protest!"

He dug his spurs into the flanks of his wretched nag and caught up with the general.

"These mountain people," he said solemnly and emphatically, "are flesh of our flesh and bone of our bone . . . *os ex osibus meis et caro de carne mea*. . . . These mountain people are carved from the same timber we are . . . from the stout timber heroes are made of."

And with a confident gesture that was as unexpected as it was bold, he pounded with his closed fist on the chest of the general, who smiled indulgently.

Did Valderrama, a crazy vagabond and something of a poet, know what he was saying?

When the soldiers came to a small settlement and desperately charged through the houses and empty huts, without finding a stale tortilla, a rotten chili pepper, or even a few grains of salt to sprinkle on the despised dried beef, their brothers who had not gone to war, some as impassive as the stone faces of Aztec idols, others more human, with sordid smiles on their greasy lips and beardless faces, looked out now from their hiding places as those fierce men, who just a month earlier had made their miserable, isolated homes tremble with fright, walked dejectedly from those huts with cold ovens and dry cisterns, their heads hanging down like dogs who've been kicked out of their own houses.

But the general did not countermand his order, and some soldiers brought in four fugitives with their arms tightly bound.

II

"Why were you hiding?" Demetrio asked the prisoners.

"We weren't hiding, *mi jefe;* we were just going along our trail."

"Where to?"

"To our hometown . . . Nombre de Dios, in Durango."

"Is this the road to Durango?"

"Peaceful folk can't travel on the roads now. You know that, *mi jefe*."

"You aren't peaceful, you're deserters. Where are you from?" continued Demetrio, watching them with a keen eye.

The prisoners became unnerved and looked at each other in confusion, unable to come up with a quick response.

"They're Carrancistas!" chimed in one of the soldiers.

That immediately restored the prisoners' self-confidence. They were no longer embroiled in the terrible quandary they'd been in since their first contact with this unknown column.

"Carrancistas? Us?" one of them answered proudly. "We'd rather be pigs!"

"The truth is, we are deserters," said the other. "We broke off from General Villa this side of Celaya, following the beating they gave us."

"General Villa, defeated? . . . Ha! Ha! Ha!"

The soldiers burst into peals of laughter.

But Demetrio's brow furrowed as if a dark cloud had just passed before his eyes.

"The son of a bitch hasn't been born who can beat my General Villa!" roared out defiantly a bronzed veteran with a scar from forehead to chin.

Without changing his expression, one of the deserters stood staring at him, and said:

"I know you. When we took Torreón, you were with General Urbina. In Zacatecas you were already with Natera and there you switched to the Jalisco contingent. . . . Am I lying?"

The effect was abrupt and definitive. The prisoners were then allowed to give a detailed account of Villa's terrible defeat in Celaya.

Demetrio's men listened to them in stunned silence.

Before resuming the march, they lighted fires to roast chunks of meat cut from a bull's hindquarters. Anastasio Montañés, who was looking for pieces of firewood among the *huizache* trees, spotted among some faraway rocks the short-maned head of Valderrama's old horse. He started shouting at him:

"Hey, come back here, you crazy fool, we decided not to shoot them. . . ."

Because Valderrama, romantic poet, knew how to get lost for a whole day whenever there was talk of shooting.

Valderrama heard Anastasio's voice and must have been convinced that the prisoners had been released, because moments later he was standing alongside Venancio and Demetrio.

"Did you hear the news?" Venancio asked him very seriously.

"I didn't hear a thing."

"Very serious! A disaster! Villa defeated in Celaya by Obregón. Carranza victorious on every front. We're done for!"

Valderrama's expression was as disdainful and aloof as that of an emperor.

"Villa? . . . Obregón? . . . Carranza? . . . X . . . Y . . . Z! What do I care? . . . I love the revolution the same way I love a volcano that's erupting! The volcano because it's a volcano; the revolution because it's the revolution! . . . But why should I care which stones stay on top or which ones get buried after the cataclysm? . . ."

And because the glare of the noonday sun reflecting off a tequila bottle flashed across his face, he wheeled his horse around and, heart bursting with joy, sped toward the bearer of such an unexpected boon.

"I like that crazy guy," said Demetrio, smiling, "because sometimes he says things that make you think."

They resumed the march, and the sense of unease was translated into a gloomy silence. The other catastrophe dawned on them quietly, but irreversibly. A defeated Villa was a fallen god. And fallen gods aren't gods. They aren't anything.

When Quail spoke, his words were a true reflection of the general mood: "Well, boys, now for sure, . . . it's every spider high-tailing it up his own thread!"

III

That small village, like all the other communities, ranches, and settlements, had been abandoned, its inhabitants streaming into Zacatecas and Aguascalientes.

So the discovery of a barrel of tequila by one of the officers was an event of miraculous proportions. The secret was guarded closely, and the men were mysteriously called to line up early the next morning under the command of Anastasio Montañés and Venancio; and when Demetrio awakened to the sound of the music, his general staff, now made up almost entirely of young ex-federal officers, notified him of the discovery, and Quail, conveying the thoughts of his colleagues, decreed: "These are hard times, and you have to make the most out of whatever comes along, because if it's true that 'some days there's water enough for a duck to swim, there are also times when he can't even get a drink.'"

The string instruments played on all day long and everyone paid his respects to the barrel; but Demetrio was as sad as could be, muttering over and over again between his teeth, *He didn't know why / and neither did I.*

In the afternoon there were cock fights. Demetrio and his senior officers sat beneath the arches of the municipal building, facing an immense weed-covered square with an old tumbledown kiosk and a few isolated adobe houses.

"Valderrama!" called Demetrio, looking up bored from the cock fight. "Come sing 'The Gravedigger' for me."

But Valderrama didn't hear him because he wasn't paying any attention to the cock fight. He was talking wildly to himself as he watched the sun go down behind the hills, vociferating solemnly: "Lord! Lord! What a great joy it is for us to be here! . . . I will set up three tents, one for thee, one for Moses, and one for Elijah."

"Valderrama," Demetrio shouted again. "Sing 'The Gravedigger' for me."

"Hey, fool, the general is calling you," said one of the officers who was sitting closer.

And Valderrama, with that eternally complacent smile on his lips, came over to Demetrio and asked the musicians to lend him a guitar.

"Silence!" shouted the gamblers.

Valderrama stopped tuning the instrument. Quail and Meco were just releasing onto the sand a pair of cocks with long, sharp blades strapped to their legs. One was dark red, with a beautiful obsidian sheen; the other had yellow wings and dark feathers like burnished copper scales with rainbow undertones.

The fight was very brief and almost human in its ferocity. As if launched by a spring, the cocks collided in midair. Necks arched and bristling with feathers, eyes bright and hard and pink as coral, combs erect and claws rigid, for an instant they held themselves aloft without even touching the ground, feathers, beaks and claws all fused into a single creature; then the red one fell back and was hurled out of the ring, claws up. The life faded from his vermillion-colored eyes, the leathery eyelids closing slowly, and his soaked plumage trembled convulsively in a widening pool of blood.

Valderrama, making no effort to restrain his expression of violent indignation, began to strum. With the first mournful chords, his anger dissipated. His eyes shone with a mad gleam. Letting his gaze drift over the square, the tumbledown kiosk, and the old adobe houses, with the sierra in the background and the flaming sky overhead, he began to sing.

He poured so much soul into his voice and played the chords on his guitar with such expression that, when he finished, Demetrio turned his face away so they couldn't see his eyes.

But Valderrama threw himself into his arms, hugged him tightly, and, with that quick familiarity he assumed with everyone at any given moment, he whispered into his ear:

"Drink them down! Those are beautiful tears!"

Demetrio called for a bottle and held it out to Valderrama.

In a gulp, Valderrama eagerly drained it halfway down; then he turned to his audience and, assuming a dramatic posture and his declamatory mode, he exclaimed with his eyes raised to the sky: "Look how the great pleasures of the revolution are captured in a single tear!"

Afterward he resumed his insane monologue, but really insane, haranguing the dust-covered weeds, the tumbledown kiosk, the gray houses, the lofty peak, and the immeasurable sky.

IV

In the distance, white and bathed in sunlight, Juchipila shone through the trees at the foot of a proud, lofty mountain, pleated like a turban. Some of the soldiers, seeing the small towers of Juchipila, sighed with sadness. Their march through the canyons had become the march of a blind man without a guide; the bitterness of the exodus swept over them.

"That town is Juchipila?" asked Valderrama.

Valderrama, just getting into his first good drunk of the day, had been counting the crosses scattered along the roads and trails, high up on the rocky escarpments, at the edges of twisting arroyos and along the riverbank. Freshly varnished black wooden crosses, crosses fashioned out of two pieces of wood, crosses made of rocks piled up and held together with mud, crosses whitewashed onto crumbling walls, humble crosses scratched onto the faces of boulders with chunks of charcoal. The trail of blood of the first revolutionaries of 1910, who had been murdered by the government. As Juchipila comes closer into view, Valderrama gets off his horse, kneels down, and gravely kisses the ground. The soldiers ride by without pausing. Some laugh at the madman, and others make mocking comments.

Valderrama, oblivious to them, recites his prayer with great solemnity: "Juchipila, cradle of the revolution of 1910, blessed land, land soaked with the blood of martyrs, the blood of dreamers . . . the only good ones!"

". . . because they never got the chance to be bad!" exclaims an ex-federal officer as he passes by, finishing the sentence brutally.

Valderrama pauses, reflects, frowns, then lets out a booming laugh that echoes through the peaks, jumps back on his horse, and catches up with the officer to ask him for a swig of tequila.

One-armed soldiers, cripples, those suffering from rheumatism and chronic coughs, criticize Demetrio. Upstarts from the city who've never even held a rifle before start out right at the top, sporting brass bars on their sombreros, . . . while the veteran tested in a hundred battles, now incapacitated for work, the veteran who started out as a simple private, is still a simple private.

And the few officers who are left from among Macías's old comrades are equally indignant, because the losses in the general staff have been replaced by slick-looking dandies from Mexico City, reeking of lotion.

"But the worst of it," says Venancio, "is that we're being overrun by ex-*federales*!"

Even Anastasio, who generally approves of everything his *compadre* Demetrio does, now agrees with the malcontents, exclaiming:

"Look, my friends, I say what I think . . . and I tell my *compadre* that if we're going to have these *federales* with us permanently, we're in bad shape. . . . Really! I bet you don't believe me! . . . But I'm not shy about speaking my mind, and I swear by the mother who bore me, I'm going to put it to my *compadre* Demetrio."

And he did. Demetrio listened patiently to what he had to say, and when he had finished, he answered him: "*Compadre,* what you say is true. We're in bad shape: the privates are griping about the sergeants, the sergeants are griping about the officers, and the officers are griping about us. . . . And we're about ready to tell Villa and Carranza to go . . . shove it . . . but I figure that what's happening to us is what happened to that peon from Tepatitlán. You remember, *compadre?* He wouldn't stop griping about his boss, but he wouldn't stop working, either. And that's the way we are: constantly griping and constantly busting our butts. . . . But that's something we shouldn't be saying, *compadre* . . ."

"Why not, *compadre* Demetrio?"

"Well, I don't know . . . just because. . . . Do you get what I'm driving at? What we have to do is keep the men's spirits up. I've got orders to return and stop the enemy from coming through Cuquío. In just a few days we're going to have a run-in with those fucking *carrancistas,* and this time we've got to smash them."

Valderrama, the vagabond poet from the royal highways who had showed up out of nowhere one day, though no one remembered when or where, must have caught something of Demetrio's words, and since there's never been a madman crazy enough to swallow fire, that very day he vanished as mysteriously as he had come.

V

They rode into the streets of Juchipila just as the church bells were ringing out noisily, merrily, with that distinctive tone that sent waves of emotion through everyone living in those canyons.

"*Compadre,* it's almost like we were back there in the early days of the revolution and we'd come to a little town and they'd ring the bells for us and the people would come out to greet us with music and flags and they'd shout 'Long live ———!' and even shoot off fireworks for us," said Anastasio Montañés.

"They don't like us anymore," replied Demetrio.

"Sure, because now we're coming back as losers, defeated and ripped to shreds!" observed Quail.

"No, that's not the reason . . . they can't stand the other guys either."

"But why should they like us, *compadre?*"

And they said no more.

They rode out onto the town square opposite the massive, rough-hewn octagonal church, reminiscent of colonial days.

The square must have been a park at one time, judging from the bare, diseased orange trees standing between what was left of the wooden and iron benches.

Once again the loud, joyful sound of bells filled the air. Then, with melancholy solemnity, the mellifluous voices of a chorus of women echoed faintly from inside the temple. To the strains of a bass guitar, the young girls of the town were singing the Mysteries.

"What fiesta are you celebrating, *señora?*" Venancio asked an old crone who was walking toward the church as fast as her legs would carry her.

"The Sacred Heart of Jesus!" replied the devout old woman, panting for breath.

Then they recalled it had been a year since the taking of Zacatecas. And they all grew even sadder.

Like all the other towns they'd seen since leaving Tepic, passing through Jalisco, Aguascalientes, and Zacatecas, Juchipila was in ruins. The black traces of fire were visible in the roofless houses, on the charred walls. Closed-up houses; here and there a store that remained open as if in jest, to display its bare shelves, which looked like the white skeletons of horses that were strewn along the roads. Hunger's frightful grimace stared out from the dirt-streaked faces of the people, from their glaring eyes which, when they fell on a soldier, blazed with hatred.

Prowling futilely up and down the streets, looking for food, the soldiers bite their tongues with rage. There's just one little café open, and they jam into it immediately. There are no beans, no tortillas: nothing but chopped-up chili and coarse salt. The officers point to their pockets crammed with bills, or cast threatening looks about, but in vain.

"Scraps of paper, great! . . . That's what you've brought us! . . . Well, try eating them! . . ." says the owner, a nasty old woman with an enormous scar across her face and a look that says *You can't frighten someone who's already lain with the dead*.

And amid the sadness and desolation of the town, while the women sing in the temple, there's no end to the chirping of the sparrows in the trees, or to the song of the linnets in the dead branches of the orange trees.

VI

Demetrio Macías's wife, deliriously happy, hurried along the mountain trail to meet him, leading the child by the hand.

He had been gone almost two years!

They embraced and stood there silently; she was overcome with sobs and tears.

Demetrio was shocked to see how his wife had aged, as if ten or twenty years had gone by. Then he looked at his son, whose eyes were fixed on him in bewilderment. And his heart leaped when he recognized the reproduction of the same steely lines of his own face and of the bright flame burning in his eyes. He reached out his arms and tried to hug him; but the little boy, very frightened, took refuge in his mother's skirt.

"It's your father, son! . . . It's your father!"

The boy buried his head in the folds of her skirt, still afraid.

Demetrio, who had handed his horse over to his orderly, walked slowly along the steep mountain trail with his wife and child.

"Thank God you've come, at last! . . . You won't ever leave us again, will you? True? It's true that you've come to stay, isn't it? . . ."

Demetrio's face grew somber.

And the two stood silently in anguish.

A black cloud came up over the mountain, and they heard the

dull rumble of thunder. Demetrio suppressed a sigh. Memories were buzzing around in his head like bees in a hive.

The rain began to fall in heavy drops, and they had to take refuge in a small cave in the rocks.

The heavy shower burst down on them, shaking the petals loose from the San Juan roses, sending them skittering through the air in starry clusters which drifted onto trees, rocks, shrubs and *pitahaya* cactuses all up and down the mountain.

Down below, at the bottom of the canyon and through the misty rain, they could see the tall, swaying palm trees, with their angular tops opening up like fans as the gusts of wind buffeted them. Mountains as far as you could see: waves upon waves of hills, then more hills surrounded by mountains which were themselves walled in by the sierra, whose peaks reached so high that their blueness vanished into the sapphire sky.

"Demetrio, for God's sake! . . . Don't go away again! . . . My heart tells me something's going to happen to you this time!"

And, trembling, she can't keep from crying.

Frightened, the child begins to wail, and she has to control her tremendous grief in order to soothe him.

The rain begins to let up; a swallow with a silvery belly and angular wings cuts obliquely through the crystalline threads of rain, which are suddenly illuminated by the setting sun.

"Why are you all still fighting, Demetrio?"

Demetrio, frowning deeply, absent-mindedly picks up a small stone and throws it down into the canyon. He stands there for a moment, staring pensively into the abyss. Then he says: "Look at that stone, how it never stops . . ."

VII

It was a perfect nuptial morning. It had rained all night, and at dawn the sky was canopied with white clouds. Wild colts with streaming manes and tails were trotting along the crest of the sierra, their spirits as high as the lofty peaks that raise their heads to kiss the clouds.

The soldiers take on some of the morning's happiness as they move slowly along the steep rocky trail. No one gives any thought to the treacherous bullet that may be waiting for him up ahead. The intense thrill of the journey consists precisely in the unforeseen. So the soldiers sing, laugh, and chatter exuberantly. The spirit of ancient nomadic tribes stirs within them. It doesn't matter whether they know where they're going or where they come from; their only compulsion is to ride, to keep riding always, never to stop; to be masters of the valley, of the high plain, of the sierra, and of everything that their eyes encompass.

Trees, cactuses, ferns—everything seems freshly washed. The rocks, their ochre hues rising to the surface like rust on old armor, shed thick drops of clear water.

Macías's men fall silent for a moment, as if they've heard a familiar noise: the sound of a shot in the distance; but several minutes pass, and the sound is not repeated.

"In these very mountains," says Demetrio, "with just twenty men, I brought down more than five hundred *federales* . . ."

And as Demetrio begins to describe that famous feat of arms, the men suddenly realize the grave risk they are running. What if the enemy, instead of being still two days' ride away, were hiding in the underbrush of that formidable ravine into which they had ventured? But which one of them would have dared reveal his fear? When did Demetrio's men ever say: *This way we'll not ride?*

And when firing starts up in the distance, engaging the advance guard, the veterans aren't the least bit surprised. But the new recruits turn tail in a desperate attempt to get out of the canyon.

A curse escapes from Demetrio's dry throat: "Fire! . . . Shoot down anyone who runs away!"

Then, like a wild beast, he roars: "We've got to drive them off the heights!"

But the enemy, hidden by the thousands, open fire with their machine guns, and Demetrio's men fall like stalks of wheat before the sickle.

Demetrio weeps tears of rage and sorrow when Anastasio slips slowly from his horse without uttering a cry and lies stretched out on the ground, motionless. Venancio falls beside him, his chest horribly riddled by the machine gun bullets, and Meco hurtles over the precipice and careens to the bottom of the abyss. Suddenly Demetrio finds himself alone. The bullets are whizzing by his ears like hail. He dismounts, drags himself over the rocks until he finds a parapet, sets up a large stone to protect his head, and chest down, he begins to fire.

The enemy spreads out, hunting down the few fugitives still hidden in the *chaparral.*

Demetrio aims, and every shot hits the mark. . . . *Crack!* . . . *Crack!* . . . *Crack!* . . . His renowned marksmanship fills him with joy; where he sets his sight, there he puts his bullet. He empties one clip and inserts another. And aims . . .

The smoke from the gunfire has not yet faded away. The cicadas chant their imperturbable and mysterious song; the doves sing sweetly from their hiding places in the rocks; the cows graze peacefully.

The sierra is dressed in its finery; over its inaccessible peaks falls a white mist like a snowy veil over the head of a bride.

And at the foot of an enormous chasm gaping open as sumptuously as the portico of an old cathedral, Demetrio Macías, his eyes fixed in an eternal stare, keeps on aiming down the barrel of his rifle . . .

 **Glossary**

cacique	Local political boss, often synonymous with the wealthiest landowner in a given area.
Carranza, Venustiano	Self-proclaimed "constitutional" leader of the revolutionary forces fighting against Victoriano Huerta. Having been a senator during the Porfirio Díaz dictatorship, he was distrusted by Pancho Villa. Carranza served as president from 1915 to 1920, was responsible for the constitution of 1917, still in force today, and was assassinated when he tried to impose his own candidate as his successor against Obregón.
cofradía	Confraternity. In Indian villages, one person is chosen each year to be in charge of the village saint or holy image. That person is responsible for throwing the party to celebrate the saint's day, and meetings of the *cofradía* would most likely be held at that individual's house.
curro	A city-bred person distrusted by the peasants.
Díaz, Félix	Dictator Porfirio Díaz's nephew. He participated in the 1913 counterrevolution against Madero but did not die in it, as Demetrio Macías announces in the novel.
federales	Government troops.
Huerta, Victoriano	Mexican general who assassinated President Madero and Vice-President Pino Suárez in 1913 and assumed the presidency. His federal army was defeated by a loose coalition of armies led by Venustiano Carranza, Alvaro Obregón and Pancho Villa and by Emiliano Zapata's guerrilla movement.
güero	A light-skinned, fair-haired individual.
jefe	Chief, leader, superior officer, boss.
Madero, Francisco	A wealthy landowner from the state of Coahuila

who campaigned for the presidency in 1910 against dictator Porfirio Díaz, who had Madero imprisoned until the election returns were favorably tabulated. Madero led the first phase of the armed revolution which resulted in Díaz's defeat and departure for France less than a year later. Madero served as president from November 1911 until February 1913 when he was brutally assassinated by Victoriano Huerta.

mochos   A term used in the mid-nineteenth century wars between Liberals and Conservatives to refer to the latter.

Obregón, Alvaro   A revolutionary general from the northwestern state of Sonora who sided with Carranza against Villa. Obregón was president from 1920 to 1924 and was assassinated by a religious fanatic in 1928 after a constitutional amendment had permitted him to be elected for a second, nonconsecutive, presidential term.

Orozco, Pascual   With Pancho Villa, one of Francisco Madero's two most important generals in the first phase of the 1910–1911 revolution against Porfirio Díaz. Later Orozco rose up in arms against President Madero but was unsuccessful.

Pintada, La   A nickname for a woman meaning "painted" or heavily made up.

El sol de mayo   Mexican historical novel published in 1868 about the French Intervention (1862–1867) by Juan A. Mateos.

Villa, Francisco (Pancho)   Revolutionary general who fought for Madero against Porfirio Díaz and later against Victoriano Huerta. He was undefeated until he was opposed by Alvaro Obregón at the Battle of Celaya. In 1916 he raided Columbus, New Mexico, in order to embarrass President Carranza and was pursued unsuccessfully by General Pershing. He was assassinated in 1923 while driving through the city of Parral, Chihuahua.

Villita   A small town in the state of Durango.

The Wandering Jew   Well-known French novel by Eugène Sue published in 1845.

Background and Criticism

The Barefoot Iliad

CARLOS FUENTES

Myth, Epic, Tragedy

The epic was viewed by Hegel as an act: an act by man who, ambiguously, detaches himself from the original land of myth, from his primary identification with the gods as actors, to engage in action himself. A self-conscious action, Hegel points out, that perturbs the peace of the substance, of the Being identical to himself: the epic is an accident, a rupture of the simple unity that epically breaks into parts and opens onto the pluralistic world of natural and moral forces.

The epic is born, writes Simone Weil, when men step out of their places and challenge the gods: Are you going to sail with me to Troy, or are you going to stay beside the tombs of Argos and Tanagra? The first victory of man over the gods occurs when he forces them to accompany him to Troy, when he forces them to travel. The epic is born from this peripeteia, this displacement or wandering that Lukács attributes to human narration. The myth—no one, among us, knows this better than Juan Rulfo—remains beside the tombs, in the land of the dead, watching over the ancestors, seeing to it that they remain quiet.

But because of its very character as voyage, as peregrination, the epic is the literary form of passage, the bridge between myth and tragedy. Nothing exists in isolation in the original conceptions of the universe, and Hegel in his *Phenomenology of Mind* sees in the epic an act that is a violation of the peaceful earth—or better, a violation of the peace of sepulchres: the epic converts the tomb into a ditch, nourishes it with the blood of the living, and in so doing convokes the spirit of the dead, who feel a thirst for life and who receive it with the self-consciousness of the epic transmuted into tragedy, aware of itself, of the fallibility and error to which it is prone and which have violated the collective values of the polis. In order to restore those values, the tragic hero returns to his home, to the land of the dead, and completes the circle in the re-encounter with the myth of origins: Ulysses in Ithaca, Orestes in Argos.

This is the great wheel of fire in classical antiquity, and its best modern theoretical interpreters – Nietzsche and Schiller in Germany, Bakhtin in Russia, Ortega and María Zambrano among us, Simone Weil in France – are in agreement that tragedy cannot propose the reconciliation of the city without three elements: the return home of the hero; the catharsis that brings about the mutual resolution of the conflicting tragic values; and the necessary time for this to occur: the transmutation, as Schiller puts it, of catastrophe into knowledge. Because catastrophe that is limited to simple destruction cannot attain the category of tragedy, writes María Zambrano: out of the destruction something must emerge to transcend it, to salvage it. In this way, as Nietzsche says, a new world, of unforeseeable superior consequences, is born from the ruins of the previous world.

In *The Iliad: Poem of Power,* in which Simone Weil spells out the lesson of the epic of our times, the Judeo-Christian philosopher tells us that the Homeric lesson has not yet ended. It is a lesson that counsels, "Never admire power, or hate your enemy, or despise those who suffer." This lesson, adds Weil, has yet to be put into practice. The *Iliad* is not from another planet merely because it is from another time. Let us remember its teaching: when man tries to extend his power to the limits of nature, he converts persons into things, violently destroys them, and cuts off their heads in the name of glory. But when glory is unmasked, it shows us that its true face is the face of death.

The value of tragedy, the value of the epic, and the value, ultimately, of myth, of the original home, the common country of the word: word and city, logos and polis. In Rulfo's *Pedro Páramo* we see the echo of the words of Jung, who accords to myth the value of original revelation of the preconscious psyche. Myths are the life of the tribe which falls into disarray when it loses its mythological legacy, like a man who has lost his soul.

This triple value – myth, epic and tragedy – depends dialectically on each of its components and on the relation among them. However, it can be posited, following Lévi-Strauss, that myth has an organizing function with respect to epic and tragedy, and consequently with respect to collective history and individuality. An organizing function, even, with regard to itself and to other myths.

In the Spanish American novel, the most successful attempt to combine epic and myth on a single narrative plane, *Cien años de soledad* (One Hundred Years of Solitude) by Gabriel García Márquez, does not achieve tragic dimension because utopia stands in the way. The Buendías are Spanish Americans; they cannot renounce hope, despite the closing words of the novel. We all know it, García Márquez and I as well: we *will* have another opportunity on earth. But we still do not know how to obtain it along the path of tragedy. We are children of the twentieth century, and tragic knowledge cannot be required of us when tragedy, in its ancient primitive centers—the West, the Mediterranean—has been replaced by crime. The history of unpunished violence, to which Rómulo Gallegos referred, is not exclusively Spanish American. It has become universal. We seek the second chance along the paths to utopia. But, above all—this is the current power of our literature—through the restoration of myth, in the sense which Gianbattista Vico gives to it: commonality of language and of history. Sustained mythic capacity will perhaps permit us one day—Lezama Lima's *Paradiso* is an approximation to it—to renew the redeeming circle of values: myth, epic, tragedy: word, action, and the collective time of culture.

For the moment, the purest mythic world in Latin America is still that of the Indians, who live myths, in the Jungian sense: they are not content to merely represent them. Antonin Artaud, in his *Journey to Tarahumara,* as well as Fernando Benítez in *The Indians of Mexico,* bear testimony to it. But our modernity makes us heirs to a religion, a politics, and a literature that undermine the triple classic value which I have just evoked.

First Christianity and then individualist and mercantilist humanism broke this great wheel of fire of antiquity and replaced it with a thread of gold and excrement: there's no reason to look back; health lies not in our origins but in our future, the transcendent future of religion, or the immanent paradise of secular engineering.

The novel, to the extent that it is a historical product of a loss—the

loss of medieval unity—and a gain—the gain of the decentered prod-
igy of humanism—is the first literary form to follow the epic in a linear,
not circular, fashion through tragedy, which reintegrates epic and
myth.

Succession, yes, but also rebellion: since its modern birth, the novel,
as if it intuited the sorrowful invocation of an absence, seeks desperately to ally itself with myth—from Emily Bronte to Franz Kafka—or
with tragedy—from Dostoyevski to Faulkner. On the other hand, it
rejects its relationship to epic, converting it—from Cervantes's *Don
Quixote* to Joyce's *Ulysses*—into an object of derision.

Why? Perhaps because the novel, being the result of a critical operation characteristic of the Renaissance that secularizes, relativizes,
and contradicts its own critical bases, first feels the necessity of ques-
tioning the literary form from which it emerged and on which it is
based, negating it: the chivalric epic of the Middle Ages, the Palatine
romance; consequently, it feels a nostalgia for myth and tragedy, but
now sensed as a critical nostalgia. Child of our faith in progress and
in the future, the novel assumes that its function is degraded if it
isn't capable of criticizing its own ideology and that, in order to do
so, it needs the weapons of myth and tragedy. Don Quixote seeks
the former at the bottom of the Cave of Montesinos; Dostoyevski,
the latter in the sediment of the czarist-papist legacy of the Third
Rome, Holy Russia; and Kafka, in the cellars of Germanic and Hebrew
fables. But Dostoyevski, Kafka, Faulkner, and Beckett also break the
future-oriented line of succession: the destinies of Ivan Karamazov,
of the land surveyor K, of Miss Rosa Coldfield, and of Malone are
no longer the same as those of Julien Sorel, David Copperfield, or
Rastignac. The latter depended completely on a headlong progres-
sion toward the future; for the former, on the other hand, destiny
has the face of simultaneous experience of time. The form of all times
is here and now, said Thomas Mann in *Jacob,* and Jorge Luis Borges
gave it a Latin American echo in "The Garden of Forking Paths":
"He believed in an infinite series of times, in a widening and dizzying net of divergent times, both convergent and parallel."

But for José Ortega y Gasset the epic has only one time, the past,
and does not admit the present as a poetic possibility. The present
time of the epic is only its being brought up to date through repeti-

tion: "The poetic theme exists previously once and for all; it's only a matter of updating it in our hearts, of carrying it to a plenitude of presence," writes the Spanish philosopher in his *Meditations on the Quixote.*

The time of the epic is an absolute but indiscriminate past. As if the epic poet were aware of the transient character of his undertaking, it hurts him to leave anything out, and he tries to fit everything into his epic sack. Ortega points out that in Homer the death of a hero occupies the same amount of space—four verses—as the closing of a door. In *Mimesis,* Eric Auerbach explains that in the epic nothing is left half-said or in half-light. The permanent foreground, the omni-inclusion, the interpolations through which the epic poet actualizes his absolute and transitional past between myth and tragedy, create that delaying sensation referred to by Goethe and Schiller in their correspondence of 1797, in which they contrast epic slowness and indiscrimination to tragic tension and selectivity.

But since the epic is no longer followed by tragedy, but by the novel, what can modern fiction offer in opposition to it, after all? In discussing Bernal Díaz del Castillo, I referred to his work as a "vacillating epic" of the chronicle of the Conquest. The adventures of the Spanish American epic tell us, in the first place, that at the moment of discovery and the Conquest, the history of the times negated the seriousness of the epic impulse. Europe was moving toward administrative centralization, a process operating in tension with the spread of commerce: the conflicts between the royal bureaucracy and the mercantile bourgeoisie would have little epic character about them. On the other hand, the events taking place in the New World called for epic treatment. Columbus, Coronado, Cortés, Cabeza de Vaca, Pizarro, and Valdivia represented an urgent demand for the epic summed up in the awestruck words of Bernal when he compared Tenochtitlán with the visions of the Amadís, and in those of Ercilla when he transformed the Araucanian chieftain Caupolicán into a kind of New World Hector. The Conquistadors set out on their journeys with what Irving Leonard calls "the books of the brave": like Don Quixote, they sought the analogy between their own glory and that of the epic poems. But behind them, in Spain, different kinds of books were announcing the new, unstable, fast-changing urban realities:

Celestina in her amatory mission as a go-between or Quevedo's Buscón in any one of his picaresque adventures in some city square experienced as many dangers and crises as Lope de Aguirre in the Amazon or Cortés on his way to the Hibueras.

The puncturing of the knightly epic by Fernando de Rojas and by the picaresque novel has no parallel in the New World other than the expedient of vacillation in Bernal's *Chronicle,* a kind of love and respect for the figure of the defeated, a lament for the vanished world which his own sword helped destroy.

For if in Europe the unique succession of classical antiquity (myth – epic – tragedy) was displaced in Croeso-Christian modernity by the succession from epic to novel, in the New World the exaggerated expectations of a utopia, its victimization by the epic, and the refuge of those expectations in a painful baroque aesthetic established at once two great traditions: the *chronicle,* which politically supports the epic version of events, and the *lyric,* which creates another world, another history capable of preserving everything destroyed and suffocated by epic history. Bernal is the secret font of the Spanish American novel: his book records, celebrates, loves, and laments, but it is offered as a "true chronicle."

Heralding the novel to come, Bernal's vacillating epic had to wait until our times to achieve, in writers like Carpentier and García Márquez, effective continuity. The delayed novel of Spanish America is no less dramatically delayed than the Spanish novel itself. Between Cervantes's *Don Quixote* (1615) and Clarín's *La regenta* (1885), more than two centuries elapsed without any peninsular novels comparable to those produced by the English or the French tradition. We were born together; we lost together; and together we must recuperate and be reborn. We were born of a vacillating epic (Bernal), which in Spain had the real reflection of the picaresque that can be opposed only by the total fiction of *Don Quixote* – so total that it exhausts itself in Spain and finds fruitful descendants only outside the country: Sterne in England and Diderot in France. We only succeeded in renewing the narrative and historical bond through a prolonged and difficult experience of *nation* and *narration* conjoined, each creating the other slowly, blindly, gropingly, ever in conflict.

Nation and Narration

I ask: to what extent is the inability to fulfill completely the Mediterranean trajectory inherent in the frustrations of our history? And to what extent is it merely a pale reflection of the modern decision, Judeo-Christian first but later bureaucratic-industrial, to exile tragedy as unacceptable for a vision of the constant pursuit of perfection and ultimate happiness of human beings and human institutions?

I choose *Los de abajo* by Mariano Azuela in order to attempt an answer, which if it has even partial validity will no doubt merely provoke a new constellation of questions. But if we approach the first hypothesis – the history of Mexico and of Spanish America, of the brave new world – *Los de abajo* offers an opportunity to comprehend the relationship between nation and narration, given the novel's amphibious nature: epic undermined by the novel, the novel undermined by the chronicle, an ambiguous and disquieting text that swims in the waters of several genres and offers a Spanish American version of the possibilities and impossibilities of those genres. Bernal's vacillating epic, Azuela's degraded epic. Between the two, the nation aspires to be a narration.

In Gallegos, or in Rulfo, we have the germination of a myth whose point of departure is the delimiting of narrative reality: in Gallegos, nature precedes it; in Rulfo, death. The myth that might rise from Azuela is more disquieting because it is born of the failure of an epic.

Nation and narration: just as the Spanish novel, or more properly the dearth of Spanish novels between Cervantes and Clarín, reveals an inability to respond verbally to the phenomenal decadence initiated during the reigns of Phillip IV and Carlos the Bewitched, the Spanish American novel, and the Mexican one in particular, could not emerge until the nation provided the contradictions and opportunities for narration expressed in *El periquillo sarniento* (The Itchy Parrot) by Fernández de Lizardi. We participate in the Rousseauistic, romantic illusion of the nation; the sentimental view derived from the reading of *Julie ou la nouvelle Héloïse,* although with a less lachrymose motive than the Colombians and the Argentines: Jorge Isaacs and José Mármol. We find the best of our nineteenth-century narrative in the adventure novels of Payno and Inclán: revolutionary preludes for Mexico, as *Facundo* and *Martín Fierro* were for Argentina. But a new quest for prestige, seen as an imperative duty, once again concealed the narrated nation behind the screen of Zolaesque naturalism. Mariano Azuela, in *María Luisa,* participates in this terrible combination of the sentimental with the clinical. A reified and predetermined world; in it the stones had no history, and fate had no grandeur: it was a dramatic pretext to encourage progress, not a totalizing vision of the past with its common obstacles and capacity for true progress, which also implies the presence of the past.

Mariano Azuela, more than any other novelist of the Mexican Revolution, lifts up the heavy stone of history to see *what there is underneath it.* What he finds is the story of the colony that no one had really narrated imaginatively before. If you stay fixed within the mere telling of "present" events in Azuela's work, without comprehending its contextual richness, you will not have read it. Nor will you have read the nation as narration, which is Azuela's great contribution to Spanish American literature; we are what we are because we are what we were.

But when I say "the story of the colony," I should have said "the tale of two colonies." Azuela is their Dickens. Stanley and Barbara Stein, colonial historians at Princeton University, distinguish several constants of that system: the hacienda, the plantation, and the social structures connected with *latifundismo;* the mining enclaves; the export syndrome; elitism, nepotism, and clientism.[1] But what is notable about these constants is that not only do they reveal the reality of the colonized country, but also they are reflected as vices of the colonizing country itself: Spain.

The tale of two colonies. A colonial nation colonizes a colonial continent. Let's sell our merchandise to the Spaniards, orders Louis XIV, for gold and silver; and Gracián exclaims in the *Criticón:* Spain is France's Indies. He might have said: Spain is Europe's Indies. And Spanish America was the colony of a colony posing as an empire.

The export of wool, the import of textiles, the flight of precious metals to northern Europe to pay for the deficit in the Iberian balance of payments, to import luxury items from the Orient for the

Iberian aristocracy, to pay for the Counterreformation's crusades and for the tasteless monuments to Philip the Second and his successors, defenders of the faith. In his *Brief on a Necessary Policy,* written in 1600, the economist González de Celorio, quoted by John Elliot in his *Imperial Spain,* says that if there is no money or gold or silver in Spain, it's because there is; and if Spain is not rich, it's because she is. Concerning Spain, González de Celorio concludes, it's thus possible to say two things that are both contradictory and true.

I'm afraid that her colonies did not escape his irony. For, what was imperial Spain's tradition if not a patrimonialism gone out of control, on a gigantic scale, so that Spain's dynastic wealth grew exorbitantly, but not the wealth of the Spaniards? If, as Stanley and Barbara Stein indicate, England eliminated every social factor restricting economic development (privileges of class, crown, or corporation; monopolies; exclusions), Spain multiplied them. The American empire of the Hapsburgs was conceived as a series of kingdoms added onto the crown of Castile. The other Spanish kingdoms were legally prohibited from participating directly in the exploitation and administration of the New World.

America was the private patrimony of the king of Castile, as Comala was of Pedro Páramo, as the Guararí was of the Ardavines, and as Limón, in Zacatecas, was of the cacique Don Mónico's.

Spain did not grow, the royal patrimony grew. The aristocracy grew, the church grew, and the bureaucracy grew so fast that in 1650 there were 400,000 edicts in force relating to the New World: Kafka in a wig. The ecclesiastical and military aggression was transferred, without resolving the problems of continuity, from the Spanish Reconquest to the Conquest and colonization of America; on the peninsula there remained a weak aristocracy, a centralized bureaucracy, and an army of rogues, thieves, and beggars. Cortés was in Mexico; Calixto, Lazarillo de Tormes, and Licenciado Vidriera stayed behind in Spain. But Cortés, the new man of the Extremaduran middle class, true brother to Niccolò Machiavelli and his politics for conquest, for change, and for the self-designated Prince who inherits nothing, was defeated by the imperium of the Spanish Hapsburgs—the absolutism first imposed on Spain by the defeat of the commune revolution in

1521 and then by the defeat of the Catholic Reformation in the Council of Trent of 1545–1563.

Spanish America was forced to accept what European modernity rejected as intolerable: privilege as a norm, the militant Church, insolent gaudiness, and the private exploitation of public power and resources.

It took Spain eighty years to occupy its American empire, according to Barbara and Stanley Stein, and two centuries to establish the colonial economy on three pillars: the mining centers of Mexico and Peru, the agricultural and cattle centers at the periphery of the mines, and the commercial system oriented to the export of metals to Spain to pay for her imports from the rest of Europe.

Mining paid for the costs of administering the empire, but it also perpetrated colonial genocide, the death of the indigenous population—which in Mexico and the Caribbean declined from twenty-five million to one million between 1492 and 1550, and in the Andean regions from six million to half a million between 1530 and 1750. In the midst of this demographic disaster, the central pillar of the empire, mining, magnified the catastrophe, exacerbating and prolonging it through a kind of slavery—forced labor. The *mita* was perhaps the most brutal expression of a colonization that first destroyed indigenous agriculture and then sent off the dispossessed to the mining concentration camps because they couldn't pay their debts.

The Rock of Ages

Brave new world: What could remain, after this, of the utopian dream of the New World as the place of renewal, where one could wash away the taint of European corruption, the garden inhabited by the noble savage, destined to bring back the golden age? Erasmus, More, Vitoria, and Vives vanish down the dark shaft of a mine in Potosí or Guanajuato; the dismal golden age turned out to be the hacienda, paradoxical refuge of those whose land had been taken away and who had been condemned to forced labor in the mine. The history of Latin America seems to have been written according to the Jesuit law of the lesser of evils, and by comparison the rich landowner was allowed to play the role of protector, patriarch, judge, and benevolent warden who demanded and obtained, paternalistically, the labor and loyalty of the peasant; in return, the peasant received from the patriarch his rations, religious consolation, and a sadly relative security. The landowner's name is Pedro Páramo, Don Mónico, José Gregorio Ardavín.

From beneath this age-old rock come Azuela's men and women: they are the victims of all the dreams and nightmares of the New World. Why should we be surprised if, when they emerge from beneath the rock, they sometimes look like insects, blind scorpions dazzled by the sun, spinning around, their sense of direction destroyed by centuries and centuries of darkness and oppression beneath the rocks of Aztec, Iberian, and republican power? They emerge from that darkness: they can't see the world clearly, they travel, move about, emigrate, fight: they go off to the revolution. They fulfill, as we shall see, the demands of the original epic. But significantly, they also degrade and frustrate them.

For *Los de abajo* is an epic chronicle that tries to shape the form of the events themselves, not of the myths, because myths cannot nourish the immediate textuality of *Los de abajo*. But it is also a novelistic chronicle that not only shapes the events but also criticizes them imaginatively.

The description of the general events is epic, even synthetic:

The federal troops had fortified Grillo and Bufa, the two peaks overlooking Zacatecas. Rumor had it this was Huerta's last stand, and everybody was predicting the fall of the city. The residents were leaving in a hurry, heading south; the trains were overcrowded; there were hardly any carriages or carts available, and hundreds of panic-stricken people were hurrying along the main road, carrying their possessions on their backs. (Pp. 32–33)

And at times he juxtaposes velocity with slowness:

Macías's horse, as if it had eagle's claws instead of hoofs, scrambled up these rocks. His men were screaming, '*Arriba, arriba!*' and following right on his heels like deer scrambling over the rocks, men and horses fused into one. Only one boy lost his footing and tumbled over the edge; the rest were over the crest in no time, storming the trenches and slashing the soldiers with their knives. Demetrio lassoed the machine guns, pulling on them as if they were wild bulls. That couldn't continue. The numerical disadvantage would have meant their annihilation in less time than it took them to get up there. But we took advantage of the enemy's momentary confusion and charged their positions with dizzying speed, routing them easily. Ah, what a fine soldier your chief is! (P. 57)

At other times, the panorama is oddly foregrounded:

From the top of the hill they could see one side of Bufa peak, its topmost crag shaped like the feathered head of some proud Aztec king. The slope, nearly six hundred meters long, was covered with corpses, their hair tangled, their clothes stained with mud and blood, and among those piles of warm bodies, women dressed in rags were trotting back and forth like hungry coyotes, turning the bodies this way and that, looking for spoils. (P. 57)

The characterization, repetitive, declamatory, heralding the qualities of the hero, is also epic: in the way that Achilles is brave, Ulysses prudent, El Cid the one who girded on his sword in a good hour, and Don Quixote the Knight of the Sorrowful Countenance, so Pancho Villa here is the Mexican Napoleon, the "Aztec eagle who has buried his iron beak in the head of the serpent, Victoriano Huerta" (p. 54). And Demetrio Macías will be the hero of Zacatecas.

But it is precisely here, at the level of epic designation, that Azuela initiates his devaluation of the Mexican revolutionary epic. Does Demetrio Macías deserve his epic tag—is he a hero, did he defeat anyone at Zacatecas, or did he spend the night before the assault drinking and wake up beside an old prostitute with a bullet hole in her navel and two recruits with holes in their heads? This novelistic uncertainty begins to take on a similarity to another epic, not the unquestioningly heroic epic of Hector and Achilles, Roland, and the Arthurian cycle, but the Spanish epic of the Cid Campeador—the only epic to start off with the hero's cheating two merchants, the Jews Raquel and Vidas, and the only epic to culminate in a malicious act of humiliation: the pulling out of Count García Ordóñez's beard—not a heroic deed but a personal insult, a vindictive act.

Demetrio Macías's rebellion also begins with an event involving a beard—that of the cacique of Moyahua—and the most violent of Macías's cohorts, the *güero* Margarito, doesn't pluck the petals from little wild flowers, but precisely from his beard: "Because I get pissed, and when I don't have anyone around to take it out on, I start yanking out my hair until I calm down. Word of honor, General! If I didn't do that, I'd die of pure rage!" (p. 65).

This is not the wrath of Achilles, but its degraded, vacillating, Spanish American counterpart: the swindles of the Cid are reproduced by Hernán Cortés, who confesses that he obtained the supplies he needed for his Mexican expedition from the inhabitants of the Cuban coast, the way a good pirate would; and such behavior bursts out vengefully in this barefoot *Iliad* called *Los de abajo*.

An epic besmirched by a history that is being staged before our very eyes—although Azuela presents it as a given—not only in the sense that the events are known by the public, but in the sense that what is known is repetitive and is fatal. However, unlike the epic, *Los de abajo* lacks a common language for its two principal characters. The comrades of Troy understood each other, as did the knights of Charlemagne and the sixty warriors of the Cid. But not Demetrio Macías and the urbane Luis Cervantes: and in this they are explicitly novelistic characters, because the language of the novel is the language of bewilderment at a world that is no longer understood; it is the sallying forth of Don Quixote into a world that doesn't look like itself; but it is also the incomprehension of characters who lack any common ground for discourse—Quixote and Sancho do not understand each other, just as the members of the Shandy family do not, nor the gypsy Heathcliff and the well-bred English family, the Lyntons; nor Emma Bovary and her husband; nor Anna Karenina and hers.

What is it, finally, that unites Macías and Luis Cervantes? Pillage, the common language of plunder, as in the famous scene in which each one, feigning sleep, sees the other stealing a jewelry box, knowing that the other is watching, thus sealing a thieves' pact of silence. The governmental pact has been formed and confirmed: cleptocracy.

The events are fatal. Valderrama declaims (p. 112):

"Juchipila, cradle of the Revolution of 1910, blessed land, land soaked with the blood of martyrs, the blood of dreamers . . . the only good ones! . . ."

". . . Because they never got the chance to be bad!" exclaims an ex-federal officer as he passes by, finishing the sentence brutally.

And events repeat themselves (pp. 66–67):

"You just . . . take it. You don't ask anyone's permission!" says La Pintada. "Otherwise, what was the revolution for? For the fat cats?" she asks. "Hell, no, now we're the fat cats!"

Criticism through Myth

"Jefe . . . . You haven't yet come to understand your true, high, noble mission. . . . It's not true that you're here just because of your run-in with Don Mónico, that cacique. You've taken up arms against the very idea of *caciquismo,* which is destroying this nation. . . ." (Pp. 35–36)

"Hell, no, now we're the fat cats!"

Strange epic of disenchantment: between these two exclamations, *Los de abajo* profiles its true historical spectre. The internal dialectic of Mariano Azuela's work abounds in two verbal extremes: bitterness engendering fatality and fatality engendering bitterness. The disillusioned Solís believes that the protagonist of the revolution is "a race that is utterly unredeemable," but he confesses that he cannot separate himself from it because "the revolution is the hurricane" (p. 51). The psychology of "our race," continues Solís, is "condensed in two words: *rob* and *kill,*" but "how beautiful the revolution is, even in its savagery!" (p. 58). And he concludes with the famous outburst: "How frustrating it would be if we who've come to offer all our enthusiasm, our very lives to overthrow a murderous tyrant, turned out to be the architects of a pedestal enormous enough to hold a couple hundred thousand monsters of the same species!" (p. 58).

But to the question, "Why are you all still fighting, Demetrio?" comes the answer, "Look at that stone, how it never stops . . ." (p. 116).

If *Los de abajo* had been relegated to an interplay between two extremes that mutually feed on each other, it would have lacked true narrative tension; its unity would be false because disillusionment and resignation are binomials that exhaust themselves quickly and end up reflecting each other, grimacing at each other like an ape in front of a mirror. For obvious reasons, critics have given too much consideration to these dramatic aspects of Azuela's work, overlooking the nucleus of a tension that bestows a vital distance between those extremes in the narrative discourse. That center of *Los de abajo* is, I repeat, what Hegel attributes to the originary impulse of the epic genre: a human act, an accident impairing the essential, a particularity that ruptures generality and disturbs the peace of the sepulchres— except on this occasion it is a novelization inserted into an epic serving the function formerly fulfilled by the epic confronting the myth that preceded it.

Azuela rejects an epic that merely reflects or justifies: he is a novelist treating an epic subject with the intention of doing it harm, to rend it asunder, to alter it by an act that will rupture its simple unity. In a certain way, Azuela thus succeeds in closing the cycle opened by Bernal Díaz: he lifts up the stone of the Conquest and asks us to look at the creatures crushed beneath the pyramids and the churches by forced labor and the hacienda, by *caciquismo* at the local level, and by national dictatorship. That stone is the stone which never stops rolling; the volcanic, hurricane-driven revolution which, in this new light, ceases to associate itself with fatality in order to assume the profile of that novelistic, human act rupturing the former epic tone that celebrates all of our historic feats and constantly threatens us with the mesmerizing norm of self-praise.

Thus what would at first sight seem to be resignation or repetition in Azuela is a critique, a critique of the historic spectre that looms over all of his characters. Saint-Just, in the midst of another revolutionary hurricane, asked himself how it would be possible to tear power loose from the law of inertia which ever leads it toward isolation, repression and cruelty: "All of the arts," said the young French revolutionary, "have produced wonders. The art of governing has produced only monsters."

Saint-Just comes to this pessimistic conclusion once he has discerned the historical passage of revolution as it asserts itself against its adversaries, destroys the monarchy, and defends itself from foreign invasion: this is the epic pattern of revolution. But then the revolution turns against itself, and this would be the tragic pattern of revolution. Trotsky wrote that socialist art would revive tragedy. He was speaking from the epic point of view and foreseeing a tragedy not of fatality or of the individual, but of class conflict and finally of collectivism. He did not know at the time that he would be one of the protagonists of the tragedy of socialism, and that this would occur in history, not in literature.

Azuela knows perfectly well the parameters of his own literary and historical experience, and this is his warning: the epic pattern of this revolution, the Mexican revolution, may well be translated into a reproduction of the previous despotism because—and herein lies the true richness of his work as a novelist—the political, familial, sexual, intellectual, and moral matrices of the old order, the colonial, patrimonialist order, have not been radically transformed. The shock of Azuela's writing is that of a ghostly premonition: Demetrio Macías (why not?) may be merely a further stage of that hostile destiny, as Hegel calls it. The microcosm for replacing Don Mónico is already there, in the band of Demetrio and his followers, his clients, his favorites, the *güero* Margarito, the *curro* Cervantes, Solís, La Pintada, Quail, ready to throw into disarray and exploit the public weal for the sake of their private appetites and to serve the whims of the Chief.

Mariano Azuela saves Demetrio Macías from that hostile destiny by a reiteration of the act that behind its fatalistic appearance resembles Hegel's epic act. The epic is a distancing of the action of man from the action of the gods. But Azuela the novelist allows his vision to transcend, in turn, the degraded epic, and to acquire ultimately the resonance of a myth. And this is the myth of the return home.

Like Ulysses, like the Cid, like Roland, like Don Quixote, Demetrio Macías left his land, saw the world, recognized and failed to recognize it, was acknowledged and ignored by it. Now he returns to the hearth, in compliance with the laws of the myth:

Demetrio strolled slowly toward the encampment. He was thinking about his yoke of oxen—two dark beasts, almost new, barely two years working the fields—and about his two acres of rich, loamy soil. The features of his young wife were stored faithfully in his memory: those soft lines and her infinite sweetness toward her husband, her indomitable energy, and her disdain for strangers. But when he tried to reconstruct the image of his son, all of his efforts were futile; he had forgotten him.

He reached the camp. The soldiers were sleeping, sprawled out between the furrows alongside their horses, whose heads hung down, eyes closed.

"The horses are all worn out, *compadre* Anastasio; it's a good idea to stay here and rest for at least another day."

"Ay, *compadre* Demetrio! . . . How I miss the mountains! If you only knew . . . you think I'm kidding, no? . . . but I don't like anything about this place. . . . I feel so sad, so blue . . . You never know what it is that's going to make you sad!"

"How many hours from here to Limón?"

"It's not just hours: it's three hard days' riding, *compadre* Demetrio." (P. 89)

Before dawn they set out for Tepatitlán. Spread out along the main road and fallow fields, their silhouettes swayed in rhythm with the slow, plodding movement of the horses, merging with the pearly tone of the waning moon, which cast its dim light over the whole valley.

Dogs barked in the distance.

"By noon today we'll reach Tepatitlán, then tomorrow, Cuquío, and then . . . the mountains," said Demetrio. (P. 90)

But Ithaca is a ruin: history destroyed it too:

Like all the other towns they'd seen since leaving Tepic, passing through Jalisco, Aguascalientes, and Zacatecas, Juchipila was in ruins. The black traces of fire were visible in the roofless houses, on the charred walls. Closed-up houses; here and there a store that remained open as if in jest, to display its bare shelves, which looked like the white skeletons of horses that were strewn along the roads. Hunger's frightful grimace stared out from the dirt-streaked faces of the people, from their glaring eyes which, when they fell on a soldier, blazed with hatred. (P. 114)

Revolutionary history strips the epic of its mythic support: *Los de abajo* is a journey from origin to origin, but without myth. And the novel then strips revolutionary history of its mythic support.

This is our profound debt to Mariano Azuela. Thanks to him it has been possible to write modern novels in Mexico because he did not allow revolutionary history, despite its enormous efforts to do so, to utterly impose itself on us as epic celebration. The home we abandoned was destroyed, and we have to build a new one. It's not certain that it's completed, says Azuela, speaking to us from that time, from 1916; it's possible that these bricks are different from those, but this whip is no different from that one. Let's not deceive ourselves, the novelist Azuela tells us, even at the cost of bitterness. It's better to be sad than stupid.

Criticism and humor, ultimately, save revolutions from the excesses of solemn authoritarianism. Azuela armed us with criticism. The revolution itself, with humor. Any revolution whose hymn celebrates a cockroach spaced out on marijuana has that, inherently.

Translated by Frederick H. Fornoff

Note

1. Stanley J. Stein and Barbara H. Stein, *Colonial Heritage of Latin America: Essays on Economic Dependence in Perspective*. New York: Oxford University Press, 1970. This is a source of information for the remainder of this section.